A SECRET SOLDIER'S CONFESSION

A NOVEL BY DENNIS BARGER

A SECRET SOLDIER'S CONFESSION

A NOVEL BY DENNIS BARGER

Published by
W.H.Wax Publishing, LLC
whwaxpublishing.com

© 2024 Dennis Barger
dennisbargerbooks.com
whwaxpublishing.com/dennisbarger

Library of Congress Control Number: XXXXXXXXXX

ISBN: 9781662960017

Proudly made in the United States of America

i

DEDICATION

I dedicate my first novel to my wife, who supported me for over forty-four years in a business career with seven relocations. Her commitment to being at my side and assuming the stay-at-home responsibilities of raising our three children was extremely important.

I would also like to thank our three kids, their spouses, and now three grandsons for giving us so much love.

Finally, thanks to all my extended family and the friends we have made over these many years. Your support and friendship have been terrific.

FORWARD

This novel is a work of historical fiction, presenting a fictional adventure narrative interlaced with various historical figures, locales, and events. Footnotes highlight these elements, offering readers insights into their historical significance. Use of these historical references serves to lend contextual authenticity to the fictional adventure. Importantly, the narrative does not validate any conspiracies about Adolf Hitler's purported survival post-World War II.

TABLE OF CONTENTS

CHAPTER ONE
Going Home

Traffic was heavy on I-95 South, leaving Annapolis. It was a clear Thursday morning in April. The sun was shining brightly, accompanied by a pleasant spring breeze.

They had delayed their departure, hoping to miss some morning commuter traffic. As usual, traffic heavily congested the southbound corridor out of Washington, DC.

Emma and Jordan were traveling to Rocky Mount, North Carolina, for the funeral service of Emma's grandfather, Henry Miller.

Emma asked Jordan, "How long do you think it will take us to get there today?"

He replied, "Probably about six hours at this pace, although we should make better time after reaching Fredericksburg."

Emma went back to her thoughts. She recalled the many summers she spent with her grandparents in Rocky Mount.

Emma grew up in Falls Church, Virginia, just outside of Washington, DC, her father, Fred Miller, worked for the federal government in the Congressional Budget Office (CBO).

Fred was the oldest son of Henry and Rose Miller. He was born in 1951, six years into their marriage. Fred attended Georgetown University and earned an accounting degree.

Fred was nearly thirty when he met Sue, Emma's mother, at a government party. They married that same year, 1981.

Four years later, they had Emma's oldest brother, Gerald, and two years hence, another brother, David. Then, in 1994, Emma, their only daughter, arrived.

Compared to her siblings and cousins, Emma was the one grandchild who consistently committed to spending the summers with her grandparents. She was not a little girl who enjoyed the kitchen and cooking activities.

However, Emma cherished going for walks and to the local shops with her grandmother, Rose. She often helped do odd jobs at Henry's furniture store and workshop. She adored her grandfather, and he loved her.

The furniture store had been in business for fifty years before Henry closed the shop. He specialized in custom furniture and wooden toys. The company thrived throughout the latter part of the twentieth century.

However, technology, mass manufacturing, plastics, and the need for more local talent eventually required closing the business.

Henry had met Rose in the fall of 1942. They were married the following summer, June 1943.

Rose's family had a long history and many relatives in the eastern North Carolina territory. Records showed her family ancestry back to 1725. Henry's ancestry revealed very little.

They had remained married for sixty-seven years until Rose's death, twelve years earlier, in 2010. They raised four children. Besides Fred, they had two daughters and another son. The daughters were both married and lived in Cary, North Carolina. Their son remains single and lives in Savannah, Georgia.

Jordan interrupted Emma's thoughts in memory with a question. "What are you thinking?"

"I was just remembering the summers with my grandparents," she answered.

She continued, "Do you remember celebrating Grandpa's one-hundredth birthday last year?"

Jordan replied, "Indeed I do. He appeared so alert and healthy."

"Yes, he was," she said. "I thought he would keep going for a few more years." She then returned to her thoughts.

Jordan looked affectionately at his wife, reflecting on her emotional strength. He knew how much she adored her grandpa, and he knew how difficult this funeral service would be for her.

Jordan recalled his first meeting with Henry. He and Emm were juniors at the United States Naval Academy six years earlier.

Jordan and his other close friends now often referred to Emma as Emm, representing her married name, Emma Miller-Murry. He and Emm were seriously dating by then. She wished to take him to Rocky Mount for a long weekend to meet Henry.

Henry lived alone, age ninety-five, healthy, spry, and alert. Jordan immediately witnessed the absolute loving affection between Emm and Henry. He, too, felt an immediate acceptance by Henry.

Jordan recalled that even at Henry's advanced age, one could tell he was a handsome young man. He was over six feet tall with a sinewy muscular build, broad shoulders, still a full head of hair, now gray, and attentive blue eyes. His mind was sharp, and his handshake firm.

Emm was five feet four inches tall, with blonde hair cut medium length just below her ears and blue eyes. Her facial features resembled those of her father, especially Henry's.

She had a round face of soft white skin, high rounded cheekbones, a small nose, a somewhat pointed chin, and small lips with straight white teeth that exhibited a beautiful smile. A head of glowing yellow hair surrounded her face.

Like her grandfather, Emm was quite athletic. During her time at the Academy, she excelled athletically, with high marks in all the physical requirements. Emm played on the women's soccer team as a forward, being the leading scorer her senior year. And like him, she was a proficient sailor.

Emm's genetics and athletic activities helped her to keep her weight near 105 pounds. Her attractive legs had a well-toned appearance, supporting a beautiful, slightly rounded butt and plump, yet proportionate breasts. She was a female whom others would say was cute.

Emm was very intelligent, graduating with a degree in Cyber Operations and a minor in German, primarily in recognition of her ancestry. They both achieved the top 10 percent of class status, graduating with distinction. He earned a degree in mathematics and a minor in history.

Jordan also played football on the Navy team. He was a lean receiver, standing six feet two inches tall. He was a standout receiver at his small Indiana hometown high school, Bloomington South.

Of course, the Navy used a running offense rather than a passing offense, so they used him more for blocking than catching the ball. One of his big glory moments was catching a touchdown in a famous Army-Navy football game.

They were in the same plebe class, but they started a relationship only in their junior year. Officially, mutual friends introduced them during the summer following their plebe year. They had just returned from completing their Command and Seamanship Training Squadron program in one of the Navy's 44 sailboats.

The Naval Academy maintained a fleet of forty-four-foot sailboats. The Navy 44 (M&R) is an American sailboat designed by McCurdy & Rhodes for United States Navy sailing training. [1]

All midshipmen must take sailing courses to develop leadership and encourage teamwork. Each boat has seven sleeping berths. Its design has a hull speed of 7.8 kn and a draft of 7.25 ft. The Navy painted all boat hulls Navy Blue; thus, all Navy veterans worldwide quickly noticed these boats.

The Academy docked all boats at the Robert Crown Sailing Center. [2]

The Academy positioned the sailing center at the Santee Basin, with an entry to the Severn River. This location allows for easy day sailing in the local bay or exiting for a full-day sail to the Chesapeake Bay and out to the open waters of the Atlantic Ocean.

All the crews were celebrating at McGarvey's down by the Dock Street harbor. It was the first time they had interacted with one another. [3]

McGarvey's was a long-standing popular Irish bar with the locals and the midshipmen. The midshipmen particularly liked that its location was just two blocks outside the rear gate, making it easy to return to the dorm when curfew approached.

They had a front bar and a back bar. Next to the back bar was the raw bar setup. Above the back bar was a loft with additional tables. Navy personnel often reserved the entire back bar area for private events, which was the case for this specific night's event.

Besides delicious food and drinks, McGarvey's was famous for a special beverage called a coffee shooter. One local who visited the bar created this concoction. It was a double-shot glass filled with Baileys, Kahlua, and coffee. One would chug the drink; it was not for sipping. It gave the person a bit of a pepping up for the night.

They each left that night with some thought of a connection. However, they waited to cement the relationship until their junior year. They had mutually returned from a one-week spring sail, each on separate sailboats.

Again, all crews were celebrating at McGarvey's. This time, they immersed themselves in mutual discussion while standing together in the back bar corner. Their first kiss occurred later that night.

They nurtured a relationship throughout their time at the Academy. Their relationship was never apparent, but intimacy was building.

Upon graduation, they were both commissioned as ensigns. Emm was first assigned to attend the prestigious Naval Postgraduate School's Center for Cybersecurity and Cyber Operations in Monterey, California. [4] She was there for nearly two years.

For her remaining three years of service, she accepted rotations to two of the five regional Cyber Centers, one in Hawaii and the other in Germany. She resigned from the Navy as a lieutenant.

As Jordan desired, the Navy assigned him to rotations on various ships. He was first assigned to the aircraft carrier, the USS Abraham Lincoln. His second assignment was a Littoral Combat Ship of the Independence class, the USS Coronado. His last rotation was a Guided Missile Cruiser of the Virginia class, the USS Texas. Each time, he received a promotion; now, he is a lieutenant commander. [5]

He remained in the Navy as an instructor at the United States Naval Academy.

Emma now works for a Department of Defense (DOD) contractor. Her work allowed her to work anywhere.

They now lived in Eastport, a neighborhood across the harbor from Annapolis and the United States Naval Academy.

Emm interrupted Jordan's reminiscence, said, "It looks like we're almost there."

Jordan answered, "Yes, the navigation says about twenty more miles."

Emm paused and sighed. "It will be good to see the family. I wish it were under different circumstances."

CHAPTER TWO
The Family Gathers

Jordan exited I-95 onto US Highway 64 East and, after a few miles, took the Falls Road exit. Soon, they were pulling into the driveway of Henry's house at 526 Falls Road.

The house was an old Queen Anne-style, painted yellow with white trim. It had a large wraparound porch. In the old days, one could sit on the porch and converse with strolling neighbors. Now, Falls Road had become a major thoroughfare, and only a few people walked by anymore.

The house still stood as one of the aristocracy's homes. Falls Road was the quintessential well-to-do area of town in the mid-1900s. Many doctors, lawyers, wealthy tobacconists, mill executives, and other successful businesspeople lived in and around Falls Road, now designated a Falls Road Historic District.

Emma's grandmother, Rose, grew up just a few houses down from the brick Colonial Revival-style house at 521 Falls Road. Her father was a doctor at the Park View Hospital, which was erected in 1914.

The hospital increased medical care in the community. Previously, medical professionals performed most surgeries in Philadelphia, Baltimore, or Richmond. Patients traveled on the 80 train to reach their destination city. [6]

At the start of the twentieth century, Rocky Mount became the northern headquarters for the Atlantic Coast Line Railroad and then quickly followed was the hospital. [7]

The headquarters created much economic development, adding to the substantial cotton and tobacco agriculture industries.

Following WWII, the city gained an attraction for pharmaceuticals, banking, and other manufacturing.

In 1942, Henry arrived in town and occupied a small rental house on North Pearly Street.

Initially, city occupants thought it strange that Henry, a strong, healthy young man, was not serving in the Armed Forces. When asked, Henry said that he was 4F, meaning he was a registrant unfit for military service because of physical, mental, or moral reasons.

The 4F designation carried quite a stigma as many thought 4Fs to be shirkers, especially when so many of their husbands, sons, and brothers accepted the request by Selective Service to be inducted into the military. [8]

He told folks that his chest x-ray had revealed a slight lung problem, which deterred him from extreme physical exertion. This explanation assuaged most people from further inquiry.

Henry initially found employment with the railroad. He mainly kept to himself, but regularly attended the one Catholic Church in the community.

The Diocese of Raleigh built our Lady of Perpetual Hope in 1939 at 331 Hammond Street. [9] Catholicism had the smallest percentage of practicing Christians in the community, with Baptists being the leading religion.

Henry first met Rose at a Sunday morning mass. She attended with her parents, two sisters, and one younger brother. He later learned her older brother was serving in the

Army. She was nineteen years old, a couple of years younger than him.

Rose wore a beautiful light blue dress trimmed in white lace at the neck and sleeves. She was a shapely girl with a trim figure. Her hair was golden yellow, and she had blue eyes and a glowing complexion.

On the second Sunday of their meeting, he mustered enough courage to ask her on a date. She bashfully agreed. Their first date was to a movie, followed by a malt and burger at the downtown diner.

They courted for nearly a year before Henry proposed to Rose. They were married in the summer of 1943. Initially, they lived with her parents, saving for a future home of their own.

The return of soldiers at the end of WWII created a massive population influx in the town, which also led to an economic boom.

Henry determined that with the increased jobs, population, and new homes, people would need furniture for these new homes.

He consulted Rose and used their savings to start a furniture manufacturing company in town. Henry secured a building at the corner of South Church and High Street.

He hired soldiers returning from the war, eager for employment and restarting their civilian lives. His business quickly prospered.

He opened a retail store in the downtown district on Southwest Main Street. This storefront allowed for a formal showroom and a more engaging atmosphere for the women to assess choices.

Then, Rose started working in the retail store, expanding into home fabrics and decorations. Together, they managed a thriving business.

In 1950, they were doing well enough to buy the house on Falls Road. The following year, Rose delivered Fred, their first child.

It was early afternoon and Jordan was about to enter the driveway when Emm perked up in her seat. She could see her parents sitting on the expansive front porch in the white wicker rocking chairs. Both waved to greet them.

Jordan parked the car and Emm jumped out the door to run to her parents. She bounded across the yard and up the three steps to hug her folks. Jordan quickly followed.

Fred and Jordan returned to the car to retrieve the luggage. Each carried two bags to the upstairs bedroom at the end of the hallway to the right. It was a medium-sized room with a high-post double bed. Henry painted the room yellow, as Rose loved the color yellow.

When Fred and Jordan returned to the porch, Emm was already making refreshing vodka tonics for her and Jordan. She carried one in each hand to the porch.

Her mother asked, "How are you doing, dear?"

Emma sighed, "I guess I am alright. I knew at Grandpa's age this time would come, but it still seems sudden."

Fred interjected, "He had a perfect life. He sure loved you, Emma; you were always his favorite."

Just then, Fred's phone rang. It was Fred's younger brother, Steven.

Fred said, loud enough for the others to hear, "Okay, we will still expect you to be here for dinner."

Fred turned to the family.

"That was Steven. The airline has delayed his connecting flight from Atlanta to Raleigh by about one hour. That means we must eat dinner later than planned, probably closer to 7:00 pm."

Sue said, "That will be fine. We only planned to grill burgers, vegetables, and a mixed salad tonight. We have an apple pie with vanilla ice cream for dessert."

The news about Steven's delay prompted Jordan to inquire, "Fred, when are your two sisters, Mary and Patricia, arriving?"

Fred replied, "Given that they both live in Cary, a short distance away, they, along with their husbands and adult children, plan to drive over in the morning for the service."

Emma asked, "What about my brothers, Gerald and David?"

Sue noted, "Both are en route now and expected to be here sometime tonight. They should be in time for dinner."

"Gerald, his wife Jean, and two sons live in Charlotte and are driving together to get here. David, who lives in Greenville, is driving with his wife and their three daughters, all of whom live in Greenville."

The arrival time gap of the other family members allowed afternoon time for Fred and Sue to have some quality checkup time with Emma and Jordan.

At about 5:30 pm, Gerald's SUV pulled into the driveway. It was a big silver GMC Yukon Denali, which offered plenty of room for the four adults and their luggage.

After the initial greetings, the two nephews, Scott and Chris, were eager to engage with Jordan. His military career utterly enthralled the boys, both teenagers. They understood and preferred the exploits of Jordan's ship service versus Emma's cyber security details.

Gerald had pursued a career in banking after graduating from the University of North Carolina. Charlotte, a prominent banking center in the Southeast, was a perfect place for him.

David arrived about thirty minutes later with his wife Beth and three daughters. They drove a Volvo XC 90. David was very safety-conscious of his girls. The girls ranged in age from Rachel, eight, Katherine, eleven, and Sally, fourteen. Unlike the nephews, all three girls admired their aunt, Emma. They loved her femininity, and that she exemplified physicality that allowed her to compete in the stereotypical male field of military service. And not to mention, she was brilliant. The girls flocked to Emma immediately upon arrival and did not leave her side for most of the evening.

David had graduated from the University of South Carolina with a degree in hospitality management. After a few years of hotel and restaurant management in the Atlanta marketplace, he opened his restaurant in the emerging food mecca of Greenville, South Carolina. His restaurant was a tremendous success.

Finally, at just near 7:00 pm, Steven, driving his Toyota Camry rental car, pulled into the driveway. Steven, who was still single after all these many years, lived in Savannah.

He was a manager with the Georgia Ports Authority. The Savannah port is one of the fastest-growing ports in the United States, and it is home to the largest single-terminal container facility of its kind in North America. Steven had worked there for years and was very instrumental in expanding the port.

Just a few years ago, Steven had finally admitted to the family that he was a gay man. He has a partner, but his partner could not get off work to attend the memorial service.

Now, all those expected to be there for the evening had arrived.

While significant, the house only had four bedrooms. Fred and Sue, Jordan and Emma, Gerald and Jean, and David and Beth would occupy those. Steven would occupy the den with a pullout sofa bed. The two boys and three girls would spend the night in sleeping bags in the spacious third-floor room with no furniture.

The family gathered on the front porch while Fred cooked burgers on the grill out back; Sue prepared the salad and other meal condiments.

Those on the porch enjoyed a few preliminary dinner snacks and beverages. They immersed each other in catching up on each other's lives.

Soon, Sue served dinner buffet style. The family ravenously ate and continued their conversations.

Following dinner, Emma and her two brothers volunteered for cleanup detail while everyone else retired again to the porch. After about two hours, everyone, a bit exhausted, retired for the evening, knowing that the following day would be more emotional.

CHAPTER THREE
The Funeral

Emma woke up earlier than usual on this Friday morning. She was already downstairs on the front porch having coffee when she heard others beginning to stir.

The early morning sun cast a beautiful sparkling glow across the front lawn. The evening cool air had left a soft covering of dew, which appeared like diamond crystals reflecting the morning sunlight. Last night, her attention focused on family, and she had not noticed the blooming flowers.

The daffodils were in bloom. They were bright yellow on long green stalks. Henry planted the daffodils in the beds, primarily near the driveway. They framed both sides of the driveway, creating a tunnel of daffodils upon entry. They had been her grandmother's favorite flower, and Henry had ensured that he maintained them in the years following her death.

The azaleas planted in front of the porch began blooming with pink and white flowers, while the crocuses planted in various beds throughout the yard created clusters of purple and orange. Those always made her think of Clemson, although nobody in the family ever attended school there.

Emma's mother shouted, "Emma, please come in to help me set up the breakfast."

Emma opened the screen door, stepping briskly towards the kitchen to help prepare breakfast for the morning. The prior night, they agreed to make it a simple buffet of fruit, bagels, and doughnuts.

Earlier that morning, Fred had gone out to the local Krispy Kreme shop before all were awake. North Carolinians loved Krispy Kreme's, especially in this area of the state. The original location was not too far away in Old Salem, Winston–Salem. They were a staple in many North Carolina homes on many mornings, and the Millers enjoyed them immensely.

The beverages would be coffee, juice, and a mimosa or Bloody Mary for the adults. Fred made a terrific Bloody Mary. He was now partial to Tito vodka and Zing Zang Bloody Mary mix, adding a healthy spoonful of horseradish, Worcestershire sauce, and Tabasco, ground pepper, and garnished with a choice of vegetables.

The adults were the first to arrive downstairs for breakfast. Fred came already showered, wearing sweatpants and a T-shirt. The other couples arrived, still unbathed. They wore their night-time pajamas or sweats and still looked groggy and unkempt.

The adults allowed the kids to sleep a bit longer. This extra slumber time gave the adults some collective time to enjoy their first morning cup of coffee, along with a start to the continental breakfast.

Jordan and Emma volunteered to wake the boys and girls upstairs, respectively. She shook the kids to get them started.

Once unhappily awake, they bounded downstairs to eat breakfast. The adults remained seated around the dining room table and the kids each took a plateful of food outside to the front porch.

Following breakfast, everyone headed to the showers for proper priming. The women wore black knee-length dresses while the men wore black or navy suits. The kids wore appropriate dress attire.

Once all was ready, they piled into their respective family vehicles. Fred and Sue rode with Jordan and Emma. Steve, being single, agreed to ride with his nephew Gerald and his family.

The church, Our Lady of Perpetual Help, was only about a twenty-minute drive. Henry had requested that there not be a visitation at the funeral home. He hated it when they did that for Rose and the funeral mass the following day. Instead, he requested a short visitation in the church rotunda, followed immediately by mass and then to the cemetery.

While en route, Sue asked Jordan, "Will we be on time?"

Jordan replied, "The visitation starts at 9:00 am, and it is now 8:15. It only takes twenty minutes, so we should be there in plenty of time."

Emma inserted, "I sure am glad we are doing everything in one day as opposed to the two days for grandma."

They arrived comfortably on time. They pulled into the church parking lot and parked each of the four vehicles adjacent.

As they exited their vehicles, Fred and Steve's two sisters and husbands arrived from Cary, North Carolina. Mary was the older of the two. Her husband Bob, along with the sister Patricia and husband Stan, rode together in one vehicle.

Mary had three children, two sons who were now living on the West Coast and would not be attending. One daughter, Laura, will arrive shortly from Raleigh.

Patricia also had three children, two of whom would not attend, as one daughter lived in Europe and a son was on a mission trip to Mexico. One son who lived on the Outer Banks was driving in and would be there in the next thirty minutes.

The church and its adjacent school building, where the Miller children attended grade school, were simple. The church was two stories in height, with exterior walls of red brick and framed in white wood trim.

A white steeple capped with gray shingles atop the roof, with a sturdy metal cross standing on top. There were six steps leading up to the entrance landing area. The front of the building had a gable roof porch covering the front entrance, supported by four white columns. Centered in the gable was a beautiful mosaic of Jesus with outstretched, welcoming hands. Double wooden oak doors opened to allow entry to the church.

Standing in the doorway, the parish priest, Father Tom, greeted the Miller family.

Father Tom said, "So good to see you all again. Henry was such a loyal parishioner. We will miss him at the church."

Fred replied, "Dad always loved being a part of this church. Do you think many people will attend the mass?"

Father Tom said, "Oh yes! Henry did not have many folks his age left, but the church members valued him. He provided so much support to the church over the years.

Did you know Henry once paid for a new roof on the church? He donated the beautiful stained-glass window high above the altar. He also provided athletic uniforms for the various boys' and girls' sports teams annually. And yes, he often provided books and classroom supplies for the school."

As the family gathered around his open coffin, they each stepped forward to pay their last respects.

When it was Emma's turn, she stood beside him, saying a quick prayer. She removed a fresh yellow daffodil from her purse, placing it on his chest beneath his joined hands. She whispered, "All my love, Grandpa. Now you will be together with Grandmother. You can both enjoy the daffodils together again."

Following Emma, each great-grandchild stepped forward to say a prayer and goodbye.

When the family finished, they stepped aside, allowing the parishioners to begin their respectful goodbyes. Over the next thirty minutes, nearly four dozen people paid their respects.

It was now almost 10:00 am. Father Tom, a prompt priest, would start mass sharply at 10:00 am. The family gathered again around the casket while non-family members took seats in the pews throughout the church.

Father Tom joined the family and asked, "Are you all ready?"

Fred, now the family patriarch, answered, "Yes, Father, we are ready to proceed."

Two altar servers stood aside from Father Tom, each holding a specific item needed for the service.

Father Tom turned to one of the altar servers and took the aspergillum, a perforated, mace-like metal ball with a wooden handle, to sprinkle holy water and to pray over the casket. He returned the aspergillum to the first server and turned to the second one holding the pall.

Father Tom took the pall, a large white cloth reminding us of our baptism, and placed it over the casket. Again, he recited a quick prayer.

Customary for a Catholic funeral mass, Father Tom walked in front of the casket, leading the procession, with the family following closely behind. Once they reached the kneeling rail crossing the church, the procession stopped. The rail had a double gate open for the priest and altar servers to walk through.

The family was now seated in the first three rows and other attendees spread themselves amongst the church pews. Collectively, the crowd created a powerful presence, and their voices provided an intense auditory rejoicing during prayer and song.

Father Tom gave a splendid sermon. He tied together service to the Lord with numerous examples of Henry's service to the church and the community over the past many years.

Father Tom completed the delivery of the traditional Catholic Mass, sure to follow all the prescribed protocols.

Communion was served, with each attendee choosing to receive it, going to the kneeling rail at the front of the church.

Father Tom addressed each recipient at the rail, placing a host, a small wafer representing the sacrificial victim, on the tongue or into the hands of the waiting recipient. One altar server held a paten, a round gold plate on a wooden handle under each person's chin. The second altar server had a tray of small cups of wine, followed by the host's receipt.

After mass, they loaded Henry's casket into the black hearse provided by the Fleming Funeral Service—the same service used for Rose upon her death. They would drive Henry to the Pineview Cemetery, east of downtown. [10] It was a short ten-minute drive across town, making it very accessible.

Family and friends would not need to search the graveyard. Henry purchased the plots years earlier, and they buried Rose there previously.

The Pineview Cemetery was the oldest and largest in Rocky Mount. The cemetery contained many prominent citizens buried there. A large granite monument carved with a family name often stood mightily guarding a set of family plots.

Henry had purchased such a monument. It was modest compared to some of the older ones, standing at about five feet tall and about thirty inches wide. It was gray with black speckled granite with the name Miller in raised block letters embossed about a third of the way from the top.

At ground level rested a granite headstone for Rose, another inscribed with Henry's name and birth and death dates. Beside those two graves, small markers identified plots allotted to all their children and spouses.

The immediate family stood nearby as the black Lincoln hearse pulled up near the gravesite. Fred, Steve, Gerald, David, Jordan, Scott, and Chris stood near the vehicle's rear, escorting the casket to the gravesite as they would be the pallbearers. Fortunately, they placed the casket on a roller cart, making it less strenuous to carry to the grave.

Once at the grave, the family and about two dozen parishioners gathered to give one last prayer. Father Tom stood near the headstone, reading Psalm 23:

"The LORD is my shepherd. I shall not want. He makes me lie down in green pastures; he leads me beside still waters; he restores my soul. He leads me on the right path, for his name's sake. Even though I walk through the darkest valley, I fear no evil, for you are with me; your rod and your staff — they comfort me. You prepare a table before me in the presence of my enemies; you anoint my head with oil; my cup overflows. Surely goodness and mercy shall follow me all the days of my life, and I shall dwell in the house of the Lord my whole life long." [11]

When done, the crowd recited the Lord's Prayer and then there was silence. Slowly, people began departing, leaving only the immediate family at the gravesite. Each one said a silent prayer and individually slipped away. The last two standing nearby were Jordan and Emm. Emm reached for Jordan's hand, intertwining their fingers. As they stood silently, Emm increased her grip on Jordan's hand. He leaned over, kissed her head and whispered, "I know. I love you."

Just then, Emma glanced down at the headstone of Henry's grave. Her eyes focused on the birth date. She noticed the carved year was one year earlier than she had recalled. This date seemed odd. She would need to ask about this later.

They soon joined the family, aside from the parked vehicles.

Sue spoke first.

"That was a lovely service. Henry would be very pleased. Now, let's all head back to the house for lunch."

They told the mass attendees they would host a lunch reception at the house. They were expecting a reasonably good turnout.

Soon after arriving back at the house, carloads of people appeared. Within fifteen minutes, there were nearly sixty people. Everyone voiced their sympathy for the family. Many people told stories about Henry's gracious support, commitment to the church and community, and excellent humor.

Bubba's BBQ, one of the long-standing local restaurants, catered lunch. It had been Henry's favorite. He knew the owner well since he had eaten lunch there most Wednesday afternoons for nearly twenty years.

The meal included ribs, pulled pork, brisket, mac and cheese, fried okra, baked beans, mashed potatoes, and garden salad.

Of course, the sauce was traditional Carolina style, containing a base of vinegar and mustard taste versus ketchup and molasses.

Dessert was a choice of red velvet cake or apple pie from a nearby local bakery.

It was nearly 3:00 pm when the last guest departed. Sue had prearranged to have a cleaning service to handle the house cleaning.

Contracting this service allowed the family time to refresh and drive to the attorney's office. The family would gather there to have the attorney read Henry's last will.

CHAPTER FOUR
The Reading of the Will

All five vehicles traveled in procession from the house on Falls Road to the attorney's office on South Franklin Street. It would take less than fifteen minutes to make the quick trip.

One by one, the vehicles turned into the Turkle, Turkle, and Jones Law office parking lot.

The law practice was one of the town's three most prominent offices, primarily representing real estate loan closings, estate planning, divorce, and family matters.

The other two more prominent firms specialized in litigation, one handling more defenses for insurance carriers and the other being a large plaintiff firm.

That firm had created a substantial litigation funding subsidiary practice, which helped increase the number of cases they could financially represent for larger mediated case resolutions or actual trial verdicts.

Henry established a relationship with Joe Turkle when he started his furniture business in 1946. Joe's son, William Turkle, joined the firm in 1968 and became a full partner in 1975.

In 1985, they brought in Sam Jones as a full partner. Joe passed away in 1987. Bill assumed the relationship with Henry.

The firm now employs two dozen employees, but Henry has always insisted that he deal directly with Bill.

The building facade was red brick, Georgian architecture. Two white columns held up a porte-cochere. Only a few vehicles pulled up under it unless it was raining.

All twenty Miller family members walked to the steps under the porte-cochere leading up to the large double oak doors.

Steven, the youngest of the now first generation of Millers, walked up to open the door. There he stood, holding it open for the others to pass through.

Fred, the patriarch, walked in first, heading straight to the receptionist's desk. There, he stated, "Hello, the Miller family. We have an appointment to see Bill Turkle."

A young man, Kevin, in his mid-twenties, replied, "Yes, Mr. Turkle is expecting you. He will be just a few minutes. Meanwhile, I will escort you to our large conference room just around the corner."

Kevin brought the family to the spacious room. It was a somewhat typical barrister's conference room. The walls were wood paneled, with bookshelves at one end, filled with many law books.

The table was a large cherry double pedestal structure with eighteen reddish brown leather chairs, one at each end and eight lined along each side. Kevin brought three additional caster rolling desk chairs for this meeting.

The room displayed certain modern conveniences and technology, specifically a larger sixty-five-inch monitor screen on one wall, conference call speakerphones at both ends of the table, outlet plugs for laptops, and an erasable whiteboard along one entire side wall, opposite a windowed lined wall out to the side street.

Once the family took their seats, Kevin asked, "Can I get anyone anything to drink, perhaps water or coffee?"

Nearly half the group asked for water, but nobody requested coffee.

Kevin left to inquire after the water beverages.

Patricia asked, "Why do you think Dad wanted us all to be together? I would have thought his estate would be simple to handle."

Mary replied, "Dad always liked to pull the family together. I'm sure this is just his last chance to request it."

Kevin returned with an armload of bottled water, handing it out to those who had asked for it.

As Kevin was leaving, Bill Turkle walked through the door, taking his open seat at the head of the table. He said, "Hello, Miller family. I certainly would like to be gathering for a different purpose. However, this is what life eventually brings to us all. Henry led a wonderful life here in this community and requested that I bring you all together to reveal his last will."

Fred told the family, "We certainly understand, and we appreciate you handling Dad's affairs all these years, as well as this last item."

Bill stated, "Then let's not delay this any longer and get on with reading Henry's will."

He then explained, "Henry made a special request that he be able to present his wishes to the family via video. We video-recorded him two years before his death, which we will play now. I have also placed Henry's verbal instructions into a formal, written legal document. I have and will provide copies to you."

Bill then asked everyone, "Please turn your attention to the monitor screen on the wall." He hit the play button on the remote keyboard in front of him.

Henry appeared on the screen. He and his attorney recorded the video two years earlier, so he looked in good health. His voice came through quite clear and strong.

Henry opened with, "Hello, family. I am uncertain which of you is present. I hope most of you are there, especially my four children, and I particularly hope that Emma is present."

Emma saw her grandfather on the screen, and hearing him say her name, she felt an immediate rush of happy endorphins streaming through her body like a wave washing over a beach. She beamed with pride, knowing Henry had singled her out on this occasion.

He paused and said, "I intend to provide you with a summary of my bequests verbally, and just as importantly, I have something to reveal to all of you, which I believe should best come directly from me and not from Bill reading it off some paper."

He further stated, "So, let's start with my bequests of physical items. I am leaving the house and all the furniture on Falls Road to all four children equally. You all can decide what you would like to do with the house. I imagine you will prefer to sell it.

A few pieces of Rose's jewelry remain in the closet safe. Mary and Patricia are to receive all of it and can decide how to divvy it up. Bill Turkle will provide you with the combination to the safe.

Also, my coin collection should go entirely to Steven in the safe, as he took a special interest in it as a child. There are three watches in the safe which should go to Fred, Bob, and Stan. Two hunting shotguns should go to Gerald and David.

I am leaving my special gold Mont Blanc pen to Emma and a letter that Bill Turkle will provide."

Again, Henry paused and stated, "Now, I want to address my financial bequests. First, I want to leave $100,000 to Our Lady of Perpetual Hope Church.

Next, I wish to leave $100,000 to the city of Rocky Mount to be used specifically for a new park and recreation facility.

I want to leave $10,000 to my five great-grandchildren, expecting each child to use it for their education. There will be $50,000 provided for each of my nine grandchildren.

Of course, my estate will pay all my funeral expenses. I will equally award all remaining funds to my four children."

Henry added, "Bill has power of attorney to liquidate all accounts into cash and disburse it as I have outlined."

Henry then gave a long pause and a deep breath.

He commented, "You all are quite special to me. I have loved you all my entire life. I hope I have provided you with nurture, guidance, and support.

As such, I feel revealing a profound secret I have guarded is important. I did not even tell Rose of this secret."

I stated earlier that Bill will provide a letter to Emma. That letter will add many more details to what I will tell you. I chose Emma because she is the best person to pursue the information in that letter.

Again, Henry paused, followed by a mighty sigh. His face displayed stress, and he was undoubtedly beginning to struggle with what he was about to say.

Henry's voice wavered and then cleared. "My real name is not Henry Miller. I was born Heinrich Müller in Munich, Germany, in 1921.

My parents were Fritz and Gertrud Müller. My father was a prominent banker. I had one older brother, two younger brothers, and a younger sister.

At age seventeen, The Abwehr recruited me. [12]

The Abwehr was a German intelligence organization responsible for surveillance, cipher, radio monitoring, and counterespionage. The Ministry of Defense secretly formed it in 1920. By 1938, the government reassigned this organization to the Oberkommando der Wehrmacht— OKW. [13]

"Vice-Admiral Wilhelm Canaris recruited me to attend Yale University in the United States for one year. [14]

While studying, I was to make a reconnaissance effort to gather information about the United States culture, people's attitudes towards Germany, and possible military efforts."

At this moment, the noise from family members was deafening.

Sue cried, "Fred, what is this about?"

And he retorted loudly, "I do not know."

Emma heard others clamoring about what they were hearing.

Jordan leaned over to Emm, whispering, "Is this for real?"

Emm whispered, "My grandfather was not one for practical jokes, so I believe this is something accurate he is telling us."

The family chatter forced Bill to pause the video.

He addressed the family. "I think we should all calm down. It will be important to hear what Henry tells you fully."

Fred chimed, "Bill, how much of this did you know and when?"

Bill replied, "I learned of this when we recorded this video. Henry and my legal responsibilities as his attorney compelled me to remain silent until today."

He added, "Now, if we are all calm, I will restart the video."

Heads nodded in the affirmative.

Once again, Henry's face and voice boomed across the room.

Henry said, "It is essential to understand that Germany was economically suffering under conditions caused by the Treaty of Versailles post-WWII.

"Hitler was already in power, bringing a newfound strength to German patriotism. [15] I was very proud to be asked to join the Abwehr."

"While attending Yale in 1938, I traveled around New England and the mid-Atlantic region, making observational notes and sending them back to Germany. I was responsible for foreign intelligence collection."

"I returned to Germany in August 1939. In September, Germany invaded Poland. [16] They sent me to train at a private estate on Quenz Lake, about forty-five miles west of Berlin. [17] The three-week training was primarily about using weapons on targets in America. We received instructions on demolition and sabotage. The training included the manufacture and dispersal of various bombs and detonators, their proper placement, and the use of their timers."

All the men attending the training class had previously visited America. We were all familiar with American money, customs, and culture and fluent in English.

We were all young men in good shape; however, we did receive some additional physical training.

As Abwehr agents, we worked on creating detailed false backgrounds for each of us. We made letters from non-existent friends and relatives, identification documents, and personal histories. We also amassed the money to be used to sustain us.

Some of our U-boat captains had surfaced off the Outer Banks, allowing crew members to rest and relax ashore briefly. The captains learned through channels that this set of cottages allowed for such safe relaxation in non-summer months.

I walked northward on the old beach road for nearly twelve miles, reaching the pink cottages in the late morning. I could walk in the open as no cars or people traveled the road.

Upon reaching the cottages, I found one identified as number two, pried the door open, and took refuge. I stayed in the cottage for almost two weeks before exhausting my food rations.

I knew that my teams of Abwehr agents were now dead, but I assumed that the other two teams of agents would land in early June, as planned.

The primary reason for setting me in the Outer Banks was that one of my early assignments was to sabotage the Kitty Hawk Radar station, AWS Station 14. [27] While holed up in the cottage, I made reconnoiter efforts at the radar station.

The radar station used the SCR-270/SCR-271 radar technology. It was a large metal antenna and transmission line standing nearly eighty feet upwards. It stood on top of a turntable assembly mounted on a trailer. The operations truck pulled the trailer. A second truck, the power truck, carried a remote generator.

Forty-five soldiers guarded the station, operating in three fifteen-member shifts every eight hours. I had devised a plan to lay charges but have yet to deploy them fully.

Instead, in early May, I made my way inland, heading to Rocky Mount. There, I would either board a train or a bus. I planned to rendezvous with the other two Abwehr teams in Cincinnati on July 4th.

I made it to Rocky Mount by May 10th, where I took up a room at a boarding house, knowing the plan for the other two Abwehr teams in early June. Both, like me, were to arrive by submarine at Long Island, New York, and Ponte Vedra Beach, Florida. The teams were unaware of my circumstances. The plan was to rendezvous in Cincinnati, Ohio, on July 4th to confirm our coordination of attacks.

I later learned some details about the two Abwehr teams.

On June 13th, traveling on U-202, George Dasch, the team leader, along with Ernest Burger, Richard Quirin, and Heinrich Heinck, landed at Amagansett, New York, a village about one hundred miles east on Long Island. Soon after landing, they encountered a United States Coast Guardsman, John Cullen. [28] They unsuccessfully attempted to bribe him. He avoided them and hurried off to make a report.

Meanwhile, the team quickly buried their supplies and uniforms. Once done, they fled to the nearest Long Island train station to travel to New York City. There, they checked into the Governor Clinton Hotel near Penn Station.

I also discovered years later that U-Boat captain Linder had unfortunately run aground while navigating the treacherous currents of the Sound. While grounded for quite some time, the rising tide came in, allowing him to pull away from the muck, and he successfully escaped to sea undetected. [29]

Later, I learned that the second Abwehr team, led by Edward Kerling along with Hebert Haupt, Herman Neubauer, and Werner Thiel, traveling in U-584, surfaced at Ponte Vedra Beach, Florida, on the night of June 18th, safely landing the team. [30]

They came ashore wearing bathing suits and military hats to avoid being mistaken and captured as spies. Once ashore, they quickly donned their civilian clothes, making their way for train travel to Cincinnati and Chicago.

I had already purchased train tickets for travel to Cincinnati at the end of June.

I did not know that Dasch and Burger hatched a plan to betray the saboteurs, defecting to the United States. Fortunately, they did not yet know of my survival, believing that I, too, had perished in the sinking of U-85.

On June 15th, Dasch phoned the New York office of the FBI to explain who he was but ended the call when the agent answering doubted his story. Four days later, he took a train to Washington, DC, and walked into FBI Headquarters, where he gained the attention of Assistant Director D.M. Ladd by showing him the operation's budget of $84,000 cash. None of the other six German agents were aware of the betrayal. During the next two weeks, the police arrested Burger and the other six. FBI Director J. Edgar Hoover did not mention that Dasch had surrendered himself and claimed credit to the FBI for discovering the spy gang. [31]

I was in the Rocky Mount train station when I heard the news about the FBI capturing a band of German saboteurs, knowing this would be the other Abwehr agents. I decided not to travel to Cincinnati. Instead, I remained in Rocky Mount until I could determine the outcome of the captured agents.

It did not take long to learn the fate of these eight captured agents.

On July 2, 1942, President Roosevelt issued Executive Proclamation 2561, creating a military tribunal to prosecute the Germans. The government placed the spies before a seven-member military commission. [32] They charged the Germans with the following offenses:

- Violating the law of war.
- Violating Article 81 of the Articles of War, defining

the offense of corresponding with or giving intelligence to the enemy.

- Violating Article 82 of the Articles of War, defining the offense of spying.
- Conspiracy to commit the offenses alleged in the first three charges.

On July 8, 1942, they held a trial in Assembly Hall #1 on the fifth floor of the Department of Justice building in Washington, DC Lawyers for the accused, who included Lauson Stone and Kenneth Royall, attempted to have the case tried in a civilian court but the United States Supreme Court rebuffed them in Ex Parte Quirin, 317 United States 1 (1942), a case that was later cited as a precedent for trial by a military commission of any unlawful combatant against the United States. [33]

The trial for the eight defendants ended on August 1, 1942. Two days later, the court found all guilty and sentenced to death. Roosevelt commuted Burger's sentence to life in prison and Dasch's to thirty years because they had surrendered themselves and provided information about the others.

They executed the others on August 8, 1942, in the electric chair on the third floor of the District of Columbia jail and buried in a potter's field in the Blue Plains neighborhood in the Anacostia area of Washington. [34]

In 1948, President Harry S. Truman granted executive clemency to Dasch and Burger on the condition that they deport them to the American occupation zone in Germany. In Germany, the citizens regarded them as traitors who had caused the death of their comrades. Dasch died in 1992 at eighty-nine in Ludwigshafen, Germany. Burger died in 1975. [35]

Realizing that if I turned myself in, I would undoubtedly face the same tragic outcome as these Abwehr agents. I remained in hiding.

Leaving the boarding house and finding a modest home on North Pearl Street to rent, I gained employment with the railroad. I mainly kept to myself other than attending church on Sunday.

When I met Rose in September, I knew she was the right girl. I knew that I needed to stay in America and must commit to a life in hiding.

You now know my true identity. I never harmed anyone or any property in the United States. I lived my life as a dedicated community citizen, a nurturing father, and a committed husband.

History has revealed that the German aggression in WWII was not a zealous patriotic cause; instead, it was a pursuit of evil.

I now conclude my revelation. I hope you all understand, forgive me, and realize the compassionate man I have been these many decades.

I love you all so very much.

"Bill will now hand you some final papers."

The Miller family mostly sat stunned. Mary broke the silence. "I am uncertain what to think. I am completely dumbfounded."

Patricia, wiping away tears, asked, "So nobody knew about this? Fred, as the oldest, not even you knew about it?"

Fred replied, "Absolutely not; I didn't know anything, I've learned about this just now."

The others all chimed in, clamoring about what they had just heard. After about five minutes, Bill Turkle interrupted and said, "Obviously, you are all a bit shocked and somewhat perplexed, perhaps even upset.

I assure you that Henry thought carefully about making the video. He concluded it was important for you to know the truth about his identity. He also thought you would all recognize and understand that his chosen life was the time in Rocky Mount with all of you."

Bill paused. "I have some papers to provide for some of you. The combination to the safe I am giving to Fred. Also, I have checks made out to each of you as recipients of Henry's financial bequests.

Once I have settled the endowment and expenses, I will liquidate the remaining accounts, sending a check for one-fourth to each of Henry's four children. Lastly, I have the letter for Emma."

CHAPTER FIVE
The Letter

Emma looked at Bill, perplexed, as she reached out to accept the letter. Other Miller family members looked on with anticipation.

As Bill Turkle handed the letter to Emma, he added another document stating, "Emma, you will need to sign this additional document. It is a bequest of your grandfather that you be the sole heir recipient of any inheritance remaining from his parents in Germany."

Emma took the second document, read it, signed it, and handed it back to Bill; she then opened the letter.

Fred proclaimed, "Emma, read it out loud. You should fully inform the entire family."

Emma looked up from the letter and said, "Of course." Then she read so everyone could hear.

Dearest Emma,

Emma, I have written this letter to you, although I am sure the entire family is listening. You are the family member most likely to embrace what you have just heard and follow my story to its conclusion.

When I left Germany, I had three brothers and a sister. The brothers are now deceased. My sister, Hilda, now eighty-four, is still alive in Munich, Germany.

Before the war, my father was a prominent banker in Munich. After the war, the bank continued to prosper as German Peoples Credit Bank (GPCB). The Marshall Plan in 1948 restructured the current bank. Under the restructuring, my father remained chairman and leading shareholder of the bank. Since the death of my father and the subsequent deaths of my two brothers, my nephew Peter now manages the bank.

Emma, I am asking you to travel to Germany to let my family know of my survival during the war, of my existence in the United States of America these past decades, and now of my death. I would like you to introduce yourself as my granddaughter, requesting a claim to my share of any family inheritance.

Bill Turkle has instructions on how to send legal notice to the family in Munich. He has several documents that will help provide proof of lineage. However, proving my true identity will be critical. There is one way to provide this proof.

When I arrived in Nags Head, I buried all my identification papers near my cottage. Later, I returned to locate the stash and took it to the Hampton National Cemetery, where I planned to bury it. I felt I must continue to hide the papers and could not even allow my attorney to keep them.

There were forty to fifty men who perished during the sinking of the U-85. Following the sinking of the submarine, there was a recovery of bodies on the morning of April 14. Rescuers recovered Twenty-nine German sailors' bodies and quickly taken to the Hampton National Cemetery, where the military buried their bodies. There, fifty-two German prisoners held at Fort Monroe prepared graves. They secretly buried twenty-nine soldiers at night with full military honors. Catholic and Protestant Chaplains each performed services.

Twenty-four sailors fired three volleys, and another military person sounded Taps. [36]

In 2004, the cemetery officials erected new headstones for the twenty-nine sailors. This event disrupted the ground, allowing me to hide my identity papers. [37]

I traveled to Hampton, Virginia, to attend the November 14 ceremony for German Remembrance Day, held annually on the second Sunday of November. That night, after the attendees departed and darkness fell, I walked to the headstone of Erich Degenkolb, one of the U-85 sailors. I buried my identity papers in a tin box about twelve inches beneath the surface. Erich's grave site is Section E-P, plot number 694, in the Hampton National Cemetery Phoebus Addition. This Section, located away from the primary national cemetery, is the resting place of many Civil War and other United States military personnel. This area is east of I-64 at the corner of West County Road and Bainbridge Avenue. It is the resting place of fifty-five German POWs and five Italian POWs from Fort Morgan during WWII, as well as the twenty-nine U-85 sailors.

You must recover these papers to present to my German family as proof of my existence, my life, and my claim to rightful inheritance. Do not seek the help of the authorities to recover these papers, as they will probably secure them for themselves, and they will tie you up in legal battles for an extended period. You must secure them secretly.

I now bring you to the last part of my story. Emma, I hope you will pursue this challenge.

Thank you.

Your loving grandfather,
Henry

Sue was the first voice to break the momentary silence. She said, "Oh my, Emma, what will you do?"

Emma replied, "I don't know. This story seems so unreal."

Jordan interjected, "Emm, we need to discuss this. Let's not be hasty."

Emm added, "I know that. It will take some time to digest this and decide whether I should pursue it. I think the best thing for now is for Jordan and me to return home to Annapolis. I'll think about this some more and I'll let you know what I decide to do."

Bill Turkle spoke, "Would you like me to start the legal notification to the family in Germany?"

Emma replied, "Yes, contact the family. I can decide whether to pursue it fully later."

Bill stated, "Okay, I will do that. I know that today's revelation is certainly a bit of a shock. I know it affects how you think about Henry and his life's secret. All I can say is that I've always known Henry to be a wonderful man, and I don't think that any of this information changes that."

He added, "That concludes the review of Henry's last request."

The family left the lawyer's office, got into their respective vehicles, and returned to the Falls Road house just after 5:00 pm. They would gather for dinner and further discuss the day's revelation. The following morning, they would all depart for their homes.

CHAPTER SIX
· The Journey Starts

Emm and Jordan had just left their small cottage home on Burnside Street in Eastport. It was a three-bedroom home with one on the main floor and two upstairs bracketing a center stairway.

The main floor also contained a small, updated kitchen and breakfast nook, a living room with a brick fireplace, a dining room, and two full bathrooms. It had a fenced backyard with a concrete patio, one large oak tree with a swing, and a one-car garage.

They had painted the house blue with white trim. On the front of their house hung three flags: the United States flag, The Naval Academy flag, and the Maritime Republic of Eastport flag.

The MRE flag was how many local Eastport residents displayed pride in their small village. It began in 1998 when the town of Eastport wanted to find a creative way to promote and encourage patronage in their village. Amicably, they tried to create independence from the Annapolis proper across the bay.

They walked nearly six blocks to the Boatyard Bar and Grill. [38] The restaurant was one of the oldest continuously operating sailor bars in the Annapolis area. It was located just a few blocks from the harbor edge, where one could stand and look across the Dock Street area.

Upon arrival, they found the restaurant overly crowded, with all inside and outside seats taken. The hostess advised that there were a couple of seats at the bar where they could order both drinks and food. They had done this before and, in fact, sometimes preferred sitting at the bar. They knew a few of the bartenders. It made ordering quicker and often more prompt.

The bar was just inside the main door to the right. It was a long L-shaped structure wrapped around the right side when standing in front. There were about ten seats, with many already occupied. They took two seats in the middle section of the bar. The bar stools were wooden, with solid backs, making them comfortable, and honey-stained wood with many coats of glossy varnish adorned the bar.

Sam, the bartender, immediately recognized them. "Welcome back. How have you been?"

Jordan replied, "Oh, just fine. We had to make a family visit to North Carolina, and now we're just getting back into our routines."

Sam handed them the menus and asked, "What can I get you to drink?"

Jordan replied, "I will have a draft, Stella."

Emm eagerly replied, "I will have a Moscow mule with Gray Goose Vodka."

As Sam went to get their drinks, they reviewed the menu for their food choices. Having been here previously, they knew most of the items on the menu.

Sam returned with the drinks. He asked, "Are you ready to order?"

They both replied, "Yes."

Emm ordered the crab cake platter. Jordan selected the daily fish sandwich.

As they waited for their food, Jordan tuned in to Emm and asked, "So, what are you thinking about the letter?"

Emm sighed and whispered, "I should honor my grandfather's wish."

Jordan quickly said, "You mean us! Anything you decide, we will do together. I am not letting you go this alone."

Emm grabbed his hand and said, "Okay, thank you."

She then said, "So, how do we go about this?"

Jordan said, "Well, I have been thinking about this. You might remember that Troy Harris, our Academy Plebe class and my teammate, is now an associate professor at Hampton University."

Emm, somewhat surprised, said, "I forgot about that. Yes, I remember him well."

Jordan said, "I thought I would call Troy, asking him if we could come down there for a reunion visit. We can probably stay at his place in Hampton. Once there, we can brief him on our real reason for being there. He might have some ideas about obtaining the documents at the gravesite."

Emm replied, "That is an excellent idea. When can we go?"

He replied, "I was thinking about the last week of May. The Academy releases for a short summer break. I think the same is true at Hampton University. Troy, likely, will be more readily available."

Emm spoke, "That sounds terrific. I can take a few days off work and drive down. You should call Troy tomorrow to check on his availability."

The following day, Jordan called Troy, eager to host them for a visit.

Troy and Jordan had been teammates on the Naval Academy football team. Troy grew up in Virginia. His parents were dairy farmers in Bedford County, Virginia. His grandfather, a black man returning from the war in Europe, used his GI muster pay to purchase one hundred acres of land in the Piedmont area of Virginia. He capitalized on Bedford County's transition from a typical tobacco-growing region to dairy.

Over the years, the family purchased an additional 200 hundred acres, making it one of the largest dairy farms operating in the county. They operated with just over 3,000 head of cattle. They were one of the most prestigious families in the county.

Troy attended Liberty High School, where he starred in football, baseball, and track. Following high school, he attended the United States Naval Academy, playing football.

After earning his engineering degree, he fulfilled his duty by deploying on multiple ships, ultimately retiring with the rank of Lieutenant Commander.

Troy earned an associate professor position at Hampton University, a historically black college. He taught classes in mechanical engineering and served in the school's Military Affairs office.

They first studied the menu, reading about each craft beer. The restaurant, known for its craft offerings, had a rotation of twenty craft brews provided. They focused on the beers offered by local craft breweries. They each selected one and ordered one when the waitress arrived.

Emma loved the hoppy flavor of IPAs. She ordered the Free Verse IPA, a 6.8% ABV from The Virginia Beer Company, Williamsburg, Virginia.

Jordan preferred Pilsners. He ordered Pils, a 5.8% ABV pilsner from Hardy Park Craft Brewery in Richmond, Virginia.

Troy liked heavier-flavored beer but was only partially into IPAs. He enjoyed Pale Ales and Lagers. He ordered the Vienna Lager, a 5.2% ABV Lager from Devils Backbone Brewing Company, Roseland, Virginia.

The waitress asked, "What size beers do you want? We offer four, twelve, and sixteen-ounce sizes."

Emma quickly replied, "The sixteen-ounce size, of course."

The two boys nodded in agreement and laughed, knowing that Emma would select the most significant size so as not to appear wimpy.

Their beers arrived in frosted glasses. They were clear but frothy on the outside, because of the glasses' refrigerated storage. Each beer had a tiny white head. They toasted to each other, swallowing a refreshing mouthful of each cold beer. Following their swigs, they focused on the food menu.

When the waitress again returned, they placed their order.

Emma informed the waitress that they would start with the baked gorgonzola flatbread. They made their flatbread of Gorgonzola cheese, caramelized onions, apricot glaze, sliced pear, balsamic reduction, and smoked sea salt.

She also ordered a Jumbo salted pretzel served with spicy mustard and house-made cheese sauce. This second item was really to appease the boys.

They each individually ordered their main lunch item. Troy selected the Meatball Sub, Sicilian meatballs on a toasted hoagie roll topped with fire-roasted red peppers, onions, red sauce, basil, and mozzarella.

Jordan ordered the WSG Burger, an eight-ounce ground Angus beef patty topped with American cheese, lettuce, tomato, pickle, onion, and house sauce.

Emma ordered the crab cake BLT with WSG bacon, lettuce, tomato, and chipotle mayo on a toasted brioche roll.

Within twenty minutes, the two appetizers arrived. They each ordered a second of the same beer and devoured the flatbread and pretzel.

Their primary food items followed about twenty-five minutes later. It was perfect timing, as they had finished the appetizers and needed another drink. They said they would keep the same selection and size.

After finishing their sandwiches, each still having some beer, Jordan whispered to Troy, "Troy, it is fantastic for you to bring us up here to Yorktown. I want to mention something important that Emm and I want to talk to you about later tonight."

Troy eagerly stated, "What exactly is it?"

Emma interjected, "Not now. We must discuss this conversation secretly. and with others out of listening distance."

Troy replied, "This sounds ominous."

Jordan said, "It is."

Troy answered, "I can't wait to hear this. Might I suggest we order the brick-oven pizzas served here instead of dining out tonight and take them back to the boat for dinner?

over the wall and entering the cemetery, which had a large canopy and would now be full of leaves at this time of year.

The tree trunk was only a few feet from the wall, and the tree canopy hung over the wall. The wall surrounded the entire exterior of the cemetery grounds.

Other Google images showed the wall to be only about three feet high and made of red brick. The picture showed a brick laid in a pattern that looked like a brick frame surrounded by a brick picture. The framing area was more expansive than the picture insert.

Each frame was about eight feet long, and about three frame sections were between a brick pillar capped with a stone pyramid element. It would be relatively easy for them to climb over this wall.

They planned to park the car under the tree. Troy would remain standing watch under the tree.

Jordan and Emma entered the cemetery, found the grave, got the documents, repaired the gravesite, and returned to Troy, where they all got in the car to leave.

They had agreed Troy should remain outside the cemetery grounds where he would serve as a lookout. He would inform them using the military communication devices each would be wearing.

Troy could also easily slip away, leaving by car, and not be subject to legal difficulties should Jordan and Emma get caught.

After properly securing the sailboat lines, cleaning the interior, and rigging the dodger over the cockpit, they returned to Troy's house.

They spent the rest of the afternoon sitting on the back deck, rehearsing their plan multiple times.

One additional concern was to find the actual location of the Erich Degenkolb grave.

Jordan first did a Google search for the Hampton National Cemetery website. Once there, he clicked the button labeled grave locator.

After choosing the cemetery and entering the name Erich Degenkolb, the site revealed the location to be Section E-P, grave number 694. It further provided a link to a view map. [41]

Upon clicking the link, the screen displayed a map of the cemetery sections. They discovered that their original site location for entry was even better because section E was beside the townhouse's parking lot.

This entry point would mean they would not need to trek across the cemetery to reach the grave.

They further determined that P represented the row number, which, by their calculation, was in the middle of the Section. Going inward a few rows would only be necessary, and the grave would be closer to the wall.

They waited until 9:30 pm to drive to the cemetery, only about twenty minutes away. That time would be late enough to allow for a cover of darkness, but not too late to raise any suspicions from the townhouse tenants.

They arrived at the townhouse parking lot just before 10:00 pm. The last parking spot near the tree was vacant, accommodating their plans.

Everyone wore dark clothes, adding additional cover. They wore long black tactical pants, sweatshirts, and stocking caps, having contemplated wearing camouflage and face paint.

Still, they chose not to, as that would cause genuine concern if someone spotted them before digging. Wearing clothing without camouflage would allow them to claim they were out for a late evening walk.

The night was clear but with no excessive moonlight, as some clouds covered the night sky and shadowed some moonlight. The air was warm but not excessively humid, which made wearing full-body clothing somewhat tolerable. There was a smell of freshly cut grass.

They checked their comms. Troy stood under the giant oak tree while Jordan and Emma climbed over the brick wall.

Jordan had a small black backpack slung over his shoulder. It contained a handwritten diagram of the cemetery section with the marked grave location.

He also had a small garden hand shovel, knowing the buried documents lay about twelve inches below the surface and would not require a large shovel.

They would pour a bottle of water on the turf to soften it for digging. They would use a piece of folded plastic to place the dirt for immediate replacement without leaving a trace of fresh dirt in the grass. Both Jordan and Emma carried a flashlight.

They noticed the grounds were meticulous. Landscapers recently cut the grass, particularly trimming all the grass at the base of the headstones. The planners laid out all the grave markers in perfect rows and equally spaced.

Each grave marker was precisely the same size, made of light gray granite, standing upright about twenty inches tall. The stonemason arched the top with smooth edging and a smooth backside.

Each front contained black block letters with the sailor's name followed by the word German and showing the birth and death date. All the U-85 headstones showed the date of death as April 15, 1945.

Their Google Maps study and preliminary research were worthwhile as they quickly found row P and the grave marker for Erich Degenkolb. Once at the proper headstone, they both promptly fell to their knees.

Jordan called over his comms, "Troy, how is it looking out there?"

Troy responds, "Everything here is quiet. Did you find the grave?"

"Yes, we are at the headstone now," replied Emma.

"We will start the digging and check back with you after we have found the documents," said Jordan.

After placing the backpack on the ground, Jordan poured water from the bottle over the ground at the base of the headstone.

Using a Ka-Bar knife, Emma traced and cut an outline through the turf to be precisely the width of the headstone and about eighteen inches away from it. She then effectively cut the root system from underneath and removed a perfect rectangle of turf. They would use this piece of turf to replace it later.

Jordan removed the garden shovel from the pack. He began digging, carefully placing all the dirt on the plastic he had unfolded and laid near the headstone. It did not take him long to dig when they heard the metal shovel tip hitting the tin can. He exhumed the canister.

Jordan pulled the tin canister from the dirt, raising it to brush off the residual dirt. The canister was about eight inches long, five inches deep, and three inches deep. The rusted, faded paint left one still able to make out the original colors, which were red, blue, and yellow.

Jordan and Emma looked each other in the eyes with surprised and excited facial expressions. Emma grabbed the tin from Jordan's hands, holding it close to her chest.

She whispered, "Oh my gosh, I can't believe it's here."

Troy then chimed in, "Did you find it?"

"Affirmative," replied Emma.

Jordan stated, "Okay, I know you are excited, but let's remain calm. Put the canister in the backpack. Let's fill the hole, clean this up neatly, and return to the car."

Jordan added, "We will open the tin box when we return to Troy's house."

Jordan replaced the dirt and packed it well. Emma laid the perfectly cut piece of turf over the fresh dirt. It looked as if no disturbance had taken place.

They confirmed they had all their gear and hurried back to the wall, where they again easily traversed it. Once on the other side, Troy was already waiting in the car's driver's seat with the engine running.

They jumped in the car, and Troy casually drove out of the parking lot and the twenty minutes back to his house. Jordan and Emma briefed Troy on their perfect exhumation exploit en route to the house.

Once inside, they gathered around the round wooden table in Troy's kitchen. Jordan removed the tin box from his pack and set it in the middle of the table.

He said solemnly, "Emm, you should be the one who opens this."

Emma embraced the tin and slid it in front of her. The lid's rust made it challenging to open. Finally, she successfully pried the lid open using a flathead screwdriver.

Emma removed a packet wrapped in tinfoil. After unfolding the tinfoil, a stack of items was visible. Emma carefully separated each item, laying them on the table for all to see.

They looked closely at each item. Their facial expressions showed complete surprise and satisfaction.

There was a small brown heavy paper bound booklet, a steel oval disc, a family black-and-white photograph, a gold ring, a 3x5 index card with two fingerprints, and a note.

Jordan picked up the brown paper booklet cover and read Soldbuch and Zuglich Personalausweis. Above the black-letter words was a black eagle with a circular wreath in its talons and the Nazi swastika inside the circle. [42]

Jordan inquisitively said, "What is this?"

Having completed some military history and German linguistics studies, Troy gave an informed response. He replied, "That is the German Wehrmacht (Army) military identification papers.

Soldbuch means military passbook, Zuglich means "at the same time," and Personalausweis means identity card; thus, a soldier's military identification and identification."

Emma, also knowing how to read and speak German, said, "I agree with your translation."

Emma asked, "What does it tell us?"

Troy took hold of the book. It was approximately 5.7 inches x 4 inches. He opened the book, scanning the pages.

He replied confidently, "Without examining every page, it shows Heinrich Müller was born in Munich, Germany. His parents were Fritz and Gertrud Müller. His father was a banker. He had one older brother, Wilhelm, two younger brothers, Hans and Philip, and a younger sister, Hilda.

He was born on June 10, 1921, and his military assignments included the Abwehr. The document also listed various dates, duty assignments, and details about his physical attributes."

Troy added, "There is no picture because, before 1943, the Germans did not include photographs.

Emma quickly stated, "It just occurred to me that Henry named my father Fred for his grandfather Fritz."

They continued to review each item on the table.

Jordan picked up the small metal disc and announced, "This looks like a dog tag."

Troy replied, "Exactly! Unlike the United States military, which issued two stamped metal tags during WWII, the German Army issued one metal tag with perforated slots along the middle. [43]

They would break the disc in half, leaving the top half with the dead soldier and taking the bottom half a record of the deceased. That is the reason both halves get stamped with the information. It has the soldier's name, birth date, military branch, and blood type. This information appears to be specific to Heinrich Müller."

Jordan asked, "Why did they call them dog tags?"

Troy responded, "Nobody knows, but the military lore is that either the United States soldiers thought they treated them like dogs or that the tags looked similar to tags on a dog's collar."

Troy added, "Did you know the Navy did not require the tags until 1917? And in WWI, they differed from the Army. Made of nickel, the Navy tags contained stamped identification information.

The biggest difference was the etched print of each sailor's right index finger on the back. The Navy included the print to safeguard against fraud, accident, or misuse. In WWII, the Navy, and all other United States military used the same tags."

Emma then held the photograph up for all to see. The writing on the back read: (*this is a family photo of the Fritz and Gertrud Müller family, 1938. The boys are Wilhelm, Hans, Philip, and Heinrich (me), and the baby is Hilda*).

Emma replaced the photo on the table, taking up the gold ring. She commented, "This looks to be a family ring. There is a crest on the face; inside, it has the initials HM and has the date of June 10, 1939.

That would be Henry's 18th birthday."

Jordan then held up the 3x5 index card and asked, "What is this?"

Troy examined it, turning over the card to read the backside. He read aloud, (*"This is the left and right index fingerprint of Henry Miller (aka Heinrich Müller).*

You can use these fingerprints to match my Wehrpass papers and civilian personal identification documents. I was required to leave these with the German military, who likely gave them to my family upon my death." [44]

There was also a short-handwritten note that read, *"You have found the authentic personal identification papers of Heinrich Müller (aka Henry Miller).*

Presenting these items to the family of Fritz and Gertrud Müller in Munch, Germany, can prove that their son survived WWII, living his life in secret in the United States of America."

Emma spoke, "Well, these items should provide us sufficient documentation to show Henry's family, proving that he is Heinrich Müller."

"I agree," said Jordan.

"So, what do you do next?" asked Troy.

"Tomorrow," said Emma, "I will contact Henry's attorney, Bill Turkle. I will let him know we have secured these identity documentation items.

I will also ask him to follow up on his prior legal contact with the Müller family to inform them as well.

Then, Jordan and I must plan a trip to Munich, Germany."

They boarded with the other business class passengers. They were unaccustomed to this, as they typically flew economy.

The business class section was at the front of the plane. It contained thirty-seven flatbed seats twenty-one inches wide, about four inches wider than the standard economy seats, which only slightly reclined. Their seats were third row A and D, adjacent seats on the plane's port side.

All seats featured a 15.4-inch HD-capable touchscreen monitor with a selection of up to seventy-five movies, over 150 TV programs, over 350 audio selections, and up to fifteen games.

They stored their backpacks conveniently overhead, settling into their comfortable personal space seats.

Emma leaned over to Jordan, said, "I've never had seats like this before, have you?"

"No. This will be quite a treat," replied Jordan.

They patiently waited for the other passengers to take their seats and then relaxed as the plane took off.

On the flight, they enjoyed an unaccustomed dinner. It included a small garden salad, bread and butter, an entrée, and dessert.

Emma selected the bowtie pasta with grilled chicken and vegetables. Jordan picked the grilled marinated skirt steak with Chimichurri sauce and potato wedges. They both had chocolate cake for dessert.

Emma commented to Jordan, "This is a delicious meal. I did not realize airline food could taste this good."

Jordan returned, "Well, now you know the difference between those who are somebody who flies and those who are nobody who flies."

Emma laughed, "Yes, we have been the nobodies."

Jordan stated sublimely, "That is for certain, but if they confirm you for Müller's inheritance, that might all change. You might fly like this forever in the future."

Emma glanced at him, somewhat surprised, and said, "You know, I hadn't given any thought about the inheritance. I've been entirely focused on proving Henry's identity."

"You will soon know," replied Jordan.

Jordan said, "I think it is time to sit back and enjoy a movie."

Emma responded, "I agree."

Jordan searched the movie selection on the seat screen until he found the new release of Top Gun: Maverick, starring Tom Cruise and a new cast of companions. He hit the play button, sitting back comfortably.

Emma had already seen the new Top Gun movie and preferred to find something else. Her search led her to Elvis. She loved Elvis' songs and was interested in watching this movie. She, too, hit the play button, reclining back to a relaxed position.

Approximately two and a half hours later, both movies finished, and they decided it was best to get some sleep. They electronically adjusted their chairs to the flat sleeping position, and each swallowed an Ambien. This would help them fully sleep until near landing time in Munich.

Emma was already awake, looking out the window at the morning light, when the pilot's voice on the loudspeaker announced their landing in the next forty-five minutes and for the flight attendants to prepare the cabin for landing.

Emma leaned over slightly to nudge Jordan awake. He was in the seat closest to the aisle.

Jordan woke up groggy from the sleeping pill, with messy hair, still desiring to sleep longer. He said, "What's going on?"

"They have announced we will be landing shortly. You need to wake up, get refreshed, and put your bed back in its seat position," Emma said sweetly.

They used the nearby lavatory to wash up, brush their teeth, and comb their hair to look presentable. Jordan, indeed, now looked refreshed.

After landing and retrieving their checked luggage at the carousel, they opened the letter containing their further instructions.

The instructions in the packet instructed them to take the S1 subway line from Munich airport to Marienplatz station. The subway would travel to the east side of Munich and arrive at Marienplatz station near the old town square. [46]

From there, it would only be a five-to-ten-minute walk to their pre-arranged hotel accommodation at the Bayerischer Hof Hotel at Promenadeplatz 2-6. [47]

The instructions informed them that the hotel was one of the luxury hotels in the old town district and was merely four locations to the west of the hotel in the same building block section at Promenadeplatz 12.

They usually would have preferred a different type of hotel. Still, the instructions said that the Müller family would pay for the hotel costs.

It was already about 9:30 am on a cloudless July day when they reached the Marienplatz station. They exited the train and went outside. The air was warm, and one could quickly tell that it would get hotter and more humid as the day progressed.

They found Weinstraße just outside the station, walking it for nearly three blocks to where they turned left on Schrammerstraße. From there, they walked about two blocks to its dead end at a small grassy area with a sign reading Promenadeplatz.

Two streets straddled both sides of the small park, creating an oval-shaped grassy park. The local tram line intersected the park with a stop directly in front of the hotel.

Upon reaching the hotel, Bayerischer Hof, they immediately recognized it as a luxury establishment. The exterior was a smooth, pale white façade six floors high. At each first-floor window hung a cobalt awning, and at the central doorway appeared a larger cobalt canopy with the same-colored curtains hanging at the sides to present a sophisticated entry décor.

Standing at the main door, ready to serve, was a handsome doorman dressed in a white shirt, indigo-colored pants, an indigo vest with gold buttons, an indigo long-tail topcoat, a matching indigo top hat with a gold band, white gloves, and shiny black shoes. The doorman tipped his hat, greeting them, "Good morning. May I assist you?"

"Yes, we just arrived on a flight this morning from the United States, and we have a reservation for a room here at this hotel," stated Jordan.

"Certainly," the doorman politely replied.

"You will find the check-in desk on the left side of the lobby. If you want to leave your bags with me and provide your name, I will ensure that a bellman promptly brings them to your room."

Jordan looked at Emm and said, "Emm, I think that's a great recommendation. Let's leave our bags with him."

Emma rolled her bag to the doorman and stated, "Thank you. The names are Mr. Jordan Murry and Mrs. Emma Miller-Murry."

Once inside, they continued to observe the opulent décor. The lobby was lengthy and broad, with white marble floor tile. Honey oak walls paneled with intermittent mirrors also adorned the lobby.

The ceiling was white, with a large stained-glass dome in the center. Merlot-colored carpet sat on the floor, along with several honey-stained oak tables and hunter-green leather low-backed chairs. A double split staircase at the far end rose to the next upper floor.

They checked in, gained access keys to the room, and traveled up the elevator to the sixth floor, where they found their junior suite room.

The room had a small sitting area, a separate bedroom with a king-size bed, and a full walk-in bathroom. There was a large window with a view over the other rooftops. It was easy to see the Frauenkirche, the famous Gothic church with iconic twin domed towers.

Their bags were already waiting for them when they entered the room. Emm said, "That's some kind of service."

"It sure is, Emm," replied Jordan.

Jordan looked at his watch and said, "It is coming up at 10:00 am; we have a meeting scheduled at 1:00 pm. Before walking to the meeting, I suggest we shower, dress, and get a bite to eat for lunch here at the hotel restaurant."

"That is a well-calculated action. I will take the first shower," Emma replied.

CHAPTER ELEVEN
The Big Meeting

Jordan had finished grooming and dressing long before Emma. He sat patiently waiting in the outer sitting room in one of the two accent chairs.

Each chair was a finely crafted subtle wingback design with intricate nailhead decorative trim and metal tips on the front wooden legs. The upholstery was gray with muted, gray-toned scrolls, soft cushioned arms, and a sumptuous cushion seat.

As Emma entered the room, Jordan stood at attention, looking impressively handsome in his gray trousers, white button-down collared shirt, navy blue blazer, and black loafers. He wore a Tag Heuer Formula 1 Quartz Chronograph steel black-face watch.

"Emma, you look quite professional," said Jordan.

Emma wore an Anne Klein Executive navy-colored pantsuit. The pants were mid-rise, with back pockets and straight legs. The jacket had a notch collar, a two-button closure, and two front pockets. A white V-neck shell blouse accented the suit. Her shoes were black leather and sleek Palmer loafers. She wore silver hoop earrings and a Tag Heuer Carrera automatic steel white face watch.

Her reply to Jordan, "And don't you look quite handsome now?"

They proceeded downstairs by elevator to the main floor. After consulting the concierge, they decided on the casual Garden restaurant. The hostess greeted them and requested a table on the sun terrace.

The sun terrace was very modern, with a sheik décor. There were three full glass walls and an entire ceiling canopy of glass. Indeed, the sun was quite prevalent.

The tables were small white quartz squares, and the chairs were wooden frames with an arched mid-back and white leather seats and back cushions.

Jordan said, "Emm, I think we should eat light since we are going to a meeting where we plan to eat heavy German food later tonight."

Emma replied, "That's a good idea. I am so looking forward to going to the famous Hofbräuhaus tonight."[48]

They placed their order with the waitress. They would both have sparkling water. Emma ordered the Dover sole with spinach and parsley potatoes. Jordan chose the Turbot with lemon emulsion and ragout of cherry tomatoes and watermelon.

Following lunch, they walked to the German Peoples Credit Bank.

A security guard asked in German, "May I help you?"

Emma responded in German, "Yes, I am Emma Miller-Murry, and this is my husband, Jordan Murry. We have an appointment with Peter Müller at 1:00 pm today."

The guard replied, "Indeed, I see you on the schedule. You can proceed to the elevator and take it to floor five. Mr. Müller's assistant will greet you at the executive lobby."

Edward greeted the couple and escorted them to the Executive conference room. The Executive conference room was up a significantly wide staircase to the sixth floor. It was the only room on the sixth floor.

The room occupied a space under the dome with windows on all sides. The dome ceiling projected a soft sky blue with white clouds, giving the feeling that one was actually under the open sky. A soft sage green painted donned the walls with darker sage green painted woodwork.

A sizeable circular mahogany conference table sat in the center of the room. The top had a sharp sheen finish, and the pedestal was a large pillar with wide feet spread at the bottom. Twelve mahogany-colored leather chairs surrounded the table. In front of every chair rested a black leather placemat and gold-plated round coasters.

A credenza served as a beverage bar stood on one wall section. A sizeable sixty-five-inch monitor screen was hanging above the credenza. The room certainly blended traditional furniture with modern technology.

Four people were already present; they stood, and introductions began.

Hilda spoke in English first and said, "Hello. My name is Hilda Snelling. Before marriage, I was Hilda Müller. Heinrich is my older brother."

Emma responded politely, "It is so nice to meet you. I am Emma Miller-Murry, Henry's granddaughter, and this is my husband, Jordan Murry."

Hilda looked quite spry for her age. She was slender, about five feet six inches, and wore her makeup and hair in a way that made her look younger than her age. Hilda wore a taupe jacket dress with scallop detail. She moved confidently and with strength. She spoke clearly, demonstrating her sharp mind.

Hilda said, "It is a pleasure to meet you both. We all speak English, so that will be the language of the meeting. I want to introduce my colleagues."

Hilda introduced the other three men in the room, said, "Allow me to introduce these gentlemen. First is Wilhelm Schwartz, our attorney; next is Hans Belcher, a fingerprint expert; and lastly is Josef Brewer, our Chief Financial Officer."

She paused, allowing each to shake hands, stating, "Peter will be with us shortly."

Just then, Peter Müller, the Bank CEO, entered through the double doorway. Two very well-built men in black suits accompanied him. The two men stepped sideways, standing at each side of the door inside the conference room.

They stood like statues. They were well over six feet tall, barrel-chested, muscular, square-jawed, and had tight-cut hair. Their eyes fixed forward, and their hands crossed below their beltline.

Peter was reasonably tall, about six feet one inch, as he was slightly shorter than Jordan. He appeared to be in his early sixties.

Peter appeared in excellent physical shape and was well-groomed. He wore a custom-made midnight blue silk suit, a white Egyptian cotton shirt, a blue silk tie with teal and pink paisley print, a solid teal silk pocket square, Ferragamo black calfskin moccasin loafers with Gancini ornament, and a Swiss Vacheron Constantin Patrimony white gold watch with a half-matte alligator strap.

He certainly looked like he just stepped off the cover of GQ magazine.

Peter immediately stated, "Hello, I am Peter Müller. You must be Emma and Jordan."

He reached out his hand and said, "So nice to meet you."

After further introductions and brief niceties, Peter suggested, "Why don't we all sit and get started?"

Wilhelm Schwartz said, "It surprised us to receive information after all these years that Heinrich survived the war. The news caused the family to be quite joyous and cautious. We reviewed all the information that Mr. Turkle forwarded. It supports your claim that your Henry Miller is our Heinrich Müller. There is, though, one item that we would like to review to gain absolute confirmation."

Emma questioned, "Certainly. What would that be?"

Wilhelm added, "We would like to compare the original fingerprint card in your possession with the fingerprints contained in Heinrich's Wehrpass identification surrendered upon entering military service."

Wilhelm looked to Hilda, and she removed the Wehrpass from her purse, passing it to Wilhelm.

Emma removed the 3 x 5 index card and handed it to Wilhelm.

Wilhelm passed both documents to Hans Belcher and stated, "Hans, would you please properly compare these fingerprints?"

Hans replied, "Certainly."

Hans scanned both documents into a portable scanner on the table. He then diverted everyone's attention to the monitor on the wall.

Hans told the group, "I have just scanned both documents using the latest Automated Fingerprint Identification System (AFIS) software version." [42]

He paused momentarily, then continued, "This software now enables us to use a dual resolution of 500 pixels per inch (ppi) and 1000 ppi. With this capability, we can fully assess all three hierarchical levels of fingerprints: patterns, minutia points, pores, and ridge contours.

Before this software version, we could only view level one and two features using AFIS. Of course, before AFIS, this was all done manually." [49]

Jordan interrupted, asked, "So, you are telling us that this software version provides a greater accuracy?"

Hans responded, "Absolutely. Unlike popular views, fingerprints are not unique to each person. When making comparisons manually, the analyst's experience and judgment played a large role in the findings. This new AFIS software removes that judgment and makes it more accurate on all three levels."

Hans then returned everyone's attention to the monitor screen.

Hans began again, "As you look at the monitor, I have both documents displayed on a split screen. On the left are the two fingerprints from the 3 x 5 card, and on the right are the two from the Wehrpass. I will now merge the two documents. You can observe that by overlaying the image on the left with the one on the right, we gain a picture of how the two images compare. The software is now performing a comparison analysis. It will take a few moments."

Hilda interjected, "This is so exciting. I am hopeful there is an accurate finding."

Emma added, "Yes, I, too, am hopeful you will find closure regarding your brother."

Hans announced, "The computer finished. The software has determined a 99.9% match with all three levels having a 98 -100% match range."

Peter asked, "Does this mean Henry Miller is Heinrich Müller, my uncle?"

Hans replied, "I am very confident they are indeed the same person."

Turning to Emma, Peter said, "Well, Emma, it appears your grandfather is my uncle and Hilda's brother."

Emma smiled and said, "Yes, what a wonderful outcome."

Peter succinctly stated, "Based upon this final analysis and the paperwork that your attorney previously sent, it also appears that you are a rightful heir to Heinrich's share of inheritance from his father."

Jordan asked, "And exactly what is that?"

Wilhelm explained, "It is somewhat difficult to determine an exact amount. There have been multiple decades of changes for the various family assets. I would like Josef, our CFO, to explain."

Josef cleared his throat, stating, "I would like to put up a document on the monitor and walk you through my calculation."

Josef then, using his laptop, switched the wall monitor to match his computer. After doing so, he briefed the group.

Josef said, "I started with an estimated starting value of Heinrich's share of family personal assets, including cash, valuables, and farmland. There also would have been a share of the stock in the bank.

I applied a simple, compounded interest amount to the value of the person's assets, reaching a number to be used. Using the number of starting shares, I calculated the increased value to today. I then converted it to United States dollars.

This value totals a handsome amount at just over fifty million dollars."

Both Jordan and Emm looked immediately dumbfounded and then smiled.

Emma said, "Oh my gosh, I had no idea it would amount to that much."

Jordan, leaning over Emma's ear, whispered, "We're rich."

Josef stated, "I will need instructions from you on how you would like this provided to you. We can transfer the total amount to your bank account, transfer funds equal to the value minus the bank stock, and issue shares. Of course, there is legal paperwork for you to sign and select an option."

Jordan asked, "How soon does Emm need to decide?"

Josef replied, "Not immediately, but we prefer it to be done soon, probably within the next few weeks."

Emma assuredly said, "Yes, I can certainly do that. I want to discuss this with a financial advisor and family back home."

Josef added, "We fully understand. Please provide us with proper addresses and other pertinent information so that we can securely mail the documents."

Hilda then politely stated, "Welcome to the family."

Emma replied, "Thank you."

Hilda stated, "I look forward to getting to know you better. I would also like to learn more about my brother Heinrich. Would you be available for lunch tomorrow?"

Emma looked at Jordan with inquisitive eyes, and he nodded yes.

Emma replied to Hilda, "Yes, we are available."

Hilda politely stated, "Oh dear, I was hoping it could be just us two girls, leaving the men out of the conversation."

Jordan quickly responded, "I understand, and Emm will join you alone for lunch tomorrow. I will find enough interesting things to do on my own."

Hilda happily replied, "Terrific. I will send a car to pick you up at your hotel at 11:30 am. We will be dining at Tantris, one of the most upscale restaurants in Munich."

The group stood and expressed pleasant goodbyes, with Jordan and Emma gleefully departing the building.

After returning to the hotel and changing into comfortable clothes, they visited some local sites before dinner. They walked to the famous Ludwigstraße, turned left, and strolled for nearly twenty minutes until they reached their primary objective: the Siegestor.

The Siegestor is a famous arch that separated Ludwigstraße from Leopoldstraße. Its architectural design rivals that of the Arc de Triumph in Paris. Its name is translated to Victory Gate, and sometimes referred to as the Triumph Arch and Peace Memorial. [50]

Jordan commented to Emm, "It is impressive."

Emm replied, "Yes, it is. I particularly like the three arches within the single structure."

Jordan said, "Okay, let's walk back to Marienplatz and then to the Hofbräuhaus for dinner."

Upon reaching the Marienplatz, Jordan asked Emm, "Don't you think we should celebrate at a finer restaurant tonight?"

Emm quickly stated, "No. We had our minds set ongoing to the Hofbräuhaus, and I'm not letting today's financial windfall change that."

Jordan apologetically responded, "Okay. Okay. I get it, and I agree. I just wanted to ensure we do what you want."

Emm, "Thank you for your consideration; now let's get some good German food and beer."

They dined on Wiener schnitzel with spätzle and sauerbraten with red cabbage and sauerkraut, while they shared an order of potato pancakes with cream cheese and applesauce.

Each person selected a beer to suit their palate. Jordan chose the Hofbräu original, a golden-colored, full-bodied, slightly malty lager. Emm desired a more robust taste profile, selecting the Hofbräu dark, with roasted malt, hoppy, and subtle malt sweetness in the finish.

After dinner, they made the short walk back to the Bayerischer Hof hotel, retiring for the evening.

CHAPTER TWELVE
Lunch with Hilda

Emma primped for her lunch meeting with Hilda while Jordan prepared his agenda for exploration alone. Emma entered the sitting room and asked, "How do I look?"

She wore a Malibu blue-and-white print wrap dress with a V-neck and length just above her knees. It slightly covered her shoulders, accentuating all of her feminine curves. She wore white casual lightweight square-toe flats. She accented her wardrobe with a gold cross necklace, diminutive diamond stud earrings in gold settings, and her Tag Heuer watch.

Jordan proudly said, "You look terrific."

Emm responded, "This is all I brought that is somewhat dressy. I didn't have time to shop for a nicer dress."

Jordan said, "You will be fine. Don't worry about it. Just enjoy the lunch and discussion with Hilda."

Emm smiled, kissed Jordan goodbye, and headed downstairs to meet the driver.

Pulling up to the restaurant, Emma saw it was more modern than the older structures nearby. It looked like a series of square, angled gray metal boxes stacked non-linearly together.

Walking through the main entrance, she noted three establishments within the building: Restaurant Tantris, Restaurant Tantris DNA, and Bar Tantris. [51]

The restaurant hostess greeted Emma. "May I help you?"

Emma stated, "Yes, I am here for a lunch appointment with Hilda Snelling."

"Certainly," replied the hostess. "Mrs. Snelling is already here. I will take you to her table."

The hostess escorted Emma to a table where Hilda sat. Smilingly, Hilda said, "I am so glad you could join me; we have so much to discuss."

Emma sat and replied, "Thank you for the invitation. I, too, am very interested in learning about the Müller family."

Before commenting further, Emma looked over the restaurant's décor.

Indeed, it was very chic. The ceiling was opulent red, and the walls were painted black, with tan carpets over dark wooden floors. White linen tablecloths draped each table. Silver utensils sat wrapped in white linen napkins, and the delicate crystal glasses stood at attention.

Standing beside each table, a yellow globe-light atop a slender silver stem pole provided ample light. The chairs were low-back, black bolstered leather.

Emma turned her attention to Hilda, said, "This is such a unique décor."

Hilda softly replied, "Yes, it is certainly different than our traditional German restaurants. The food here is very haute cuisine."

She paused and added, "For lunch, the prix fixe menu offers a choice of four or six courses. I will have you choose after you have looked at the menu for today."

Emma directed her attention to the menu.

4/6 Courses

ARDIN Mullet · Cucumber · Verbena

RIVIÈRE Salmon Trout · Dill · Sauce Normande

PETIT BATEAU Red Mullet · Bell Pepper · Sobrassada

LA FERME Veal · Black Pudding · Mustard

BAVIÈRE Kiwi · Mint · Ginger

FIN D'ÉTÉ Plum · Shiso · Rice

Four-course-menu Main course by choice PETIT BATEAU or LA FERME and without BAVIÈR

She raised her eyes to Hilda, said, "Let's go all in on the six-course menu."

Hilda replied, "I hoped that would be your choice."

When the waiter arrived, Hilda placed the order for the six-course menu. She also ordered a bottle of 2017 Riesling "G-Max," Klaus-Peter Keller, Rheinhessen, Deutschland.

Over lunch, they took turns asking questions and providing answers. It was like watching a tennis match, with one person answering the question and the other answering. Then, they would switch sides and repeat the process.

Emma started, "What can you tell me about the Müller family and Henry?"

"I remember very little about him, as I was young when he left. I can tell you that our parents were very loving people. Father was strict but kind. He worked as a banker, which regarded us as a well-to-do family.

Mother was a pretty woman. She stayed at home raising four children and attending the proper social activities of the day," Hilda proudly stated.

She continued, "Henry was the third child with two older brothers, Hans and Philip, and me, his younger sister. Hans and Philip both served in the military during the war. Hans returned, but Philip did not.

Our devastated mother lost two sons, Philip and Heinrich, in the war. Hans was married in early 1940 before going off to war. His wife, Matilda, was already pregnant and giving birth to a son late that year.

That son, Johan, married early at age twenty-two, and he, too, immediately had a son, Peter. Hans eventually also became the bank president, but Johan never achieved such, dying early on from cancer.

As you know, Peter is now the bank CEO."

"Are there any other living Müller family members?" asked Emma.

"I am a widow with two daughters still alive. They each have husbands, and I have five adult grandchildren. Two of them are married.

Hans had a daughter, besides Johan. She was married with three living children and now two grandchildren.

Aside from Peter, Johan had a daughter and another son. The son died as a teenager in a tragic automobile accident. The daughter is married with no children," added Hilda.

Hilda then asked, "What can you tell me about Heinrich?"

Emma responded, "He was the most special grandfather to me. He married Rose, a local girl in Rocky Mount, North Carolina, where they settled together to raise a family and run a furniture business."

"What about children?" asked Hilda.

"Yes," replied Emma. "They had four children: a son, Fred, my father. He married Sue. They also had two daughters, each married, and another son, Steven, who has a partner. Including me, there are twelve grandchildren."

"And what kind of man was Henry?" asked Hilda.

"Oh, he was such a loving and kind man," Emma said with a prideful, glowing face. "He raised his children with solid discipline but showered them with love and encouragement.

His wife and grandchildren meant the world to him and he lived dedicated to her and embraced his grandchildren. I must confess that he especially favored me.

His philanthropy extended to the community and his church."

Emma then inquired, "Where did you all live?"

"We had a fine house in the city of Munich. We could walk to school and the shops. On a fine weather day, Father would sometimes walk to the bank, or he could take a trolley.

We also had a mountain retreat. It had beautiful views of the Bavarian mountains south of Munich. Mother and I went to live there near the end of the war.

The war destroyed the house. We still have the mountain retreat in the family," stated Hilda.

"And which family members are currently involved with the bank?" asked Emma.

Hilda responded, "Peter is the CEO, and I am on the board of directors. However, no other living family members are directly involved. Some of them still own some stock in the bank."

They continued asking each other questions and providing answers for nearly two hours. Hilda provided a substantial amount of information about Müller's family history and information about the bank.

Emma responded with a complete history of Henry's life in the United States, including his marriage, Miller family members, business, and philanthropy. Their conversion long exceeded food consumption and a second bottle of wine.

Nearly done, Hilda leaned in close and whispered, "Emma, I feel God brought you to me in my final years as an answer to my many years of prayer."

Emma, somewhat confused, asked, "What do you mean?"

Hilda continued, "I have long thought that after the war, the bank remained involved with the ongoing secret Nazi Party. I think Peter knows something about it."

Emma asked, "Have you ever confronted him about it?"

"No, I would feel undignified," responded Hilda.

Emma asked, "Why are you telling me this?"

Hilda answered, "Because I am old and will not be here forever. I want somebody to know about my concern. Who is better than a young, next-generation family member? And besides, I want you to be careful regarding your involvement with the bank."

Emma leaned close and confidently stated, "I appreciate your trust in telling me this, however, and I do not know what I can or should do about it."

"Do nothing," said Hilda.

Hilda settled the bill with the waiter. The two women moved to the main entrance lobby, where they embraced. They promised to keep in regular contact. Hilda departed in her car, and Emma left in hers, heading back to the hotel to join Jordan.

CHAPTER THIRTEEN
Justification of Action

Emma sat in their hotel bedroom's sitting area, waiting for Jordan to return from sightseeing. She was stewing over whether to tell Jordan about Hilda's secret suspicion.

Jordan entered the room excitedly to tell Emm about all the sights he experienced for the day. However, he immediately noticed that Emm seemed worried. After closing the door, he asked, "What's wrong? What happened at lunch?"

Emm answered, "Lunch was fabulous, and the restaurant was divine. I learned so much about the Müller family. It would please me to learn they did so well after the war."

Jordan interrupted, "Sounds wonderful, so what's the trouble?"

Emm said, "Well, Hilda shared a personal suspicion that disturbed me."

"What suspicion?" asked Jordan.

Emm added, "She suspects that the bank and perhaps now Peter still have ties to the Nazi Party."

Jordan replied, astounded, "How is that possible?"

Emma said assuredly, "I don't know, but I mean to find out."

"And just how do you propose to do that?" Jordan asked in a tone of doubt.

With conviction, Emma stated, "I have been sitting here giving it a lot of thought. I think I should try to breach the firewall to the bank's computer system and snoop around in their files."

Jordan said loudly and defiantly, "You can't do that; it's illegal."

Emm firmly states, "I know, but it's the only thing I know to do."

Jordan replied emphatically, "Emm, you took an oath as an officer in the Navy, which I still abide by today."

He paused momentarily and quickly added, let me recite it again for you,

"I, Jordan Miller, having been appointed an officer in the Navy of the United States, as stated in the grade of Lieutenant Commander, do solemnly swear that I will support and defend the Constitution of the United States against all enemies, foreign or domestic, that I will bear true faith and allegiance to the same; that I take this obligation freely, without any mental reservations or purpose of evasion; and that I will well and faithfully discharge the duties of the office upon which I am about to enter; So help me God." [52]

He paused again, looking directly at Emm, "Do you remember this? You took the same oath."

Emm responded, "I do, and I recognize that what I am suggesting is illegal. But, at the same time, I also believe that in doing so, I am upholding my oath as the Nazi Party was, and still is, an enemy of my country."

"That's an interesting perspective," said Jordan.

Emm added, "And, even though Henry never committed an act of aggression in the United States, I think I need to do something in his honor to right any wrongs committed by his family."

"Okay, you have convinced me. I will support you," said Jordan. "When and how do you propose to do this?"

Emm responded, "I have my computer with me, so that we can do this right now from here in the hotel room."

Emm and Jordan gathered at the small desk in the room, both seated in chairs, eyeing the laptop computer screen. Jordan watched Emm skillfully strike keys, making what looked like progress in her effort to gain access to the bank's computer system.

Emm was an expert in cyber security. It took her about thirty-five minutes to breach the firewall of the bank's system. "I think I'm in now."

Jordan looked at her and said, "Great, now what?"

Emm said, "I'm not sure, but I think it would be best to start with Peter's files and see what that gives us."

Emm spent the next ninety minutes tracking through Peter's files when she found one with an odd file name and password protected. She turned to Jordan. "This file name seems odd."

"What is it?" he asked.

"The file name is Neun, password-protected," she said.

Jordan added, "Even I know that Neun is the German word for the number nine."

"Yes, but how do I access it? This file might shed some light on the matter," she said.

Jordan said, "Let me think about it; meanwhile, you keep looking for other files."

After spending time in the chair thinking and scratching notes on paper, Jordan returned with a proclamation, "I think I might have solved the password issue for that file!"

"Do tell," said Emm.

Jordan proudly informed her, "There is a theory that the square of any odd integer minus one is divisible by eight. So, the number nine is an odd integer; its square is 3 x 3; thus, nine minus one equals eight, and that number obviously can be 1 x 8 or 8 x 1. [53]

If you choose 1 x 8 and then use each number to correspond to the alphabet, you get the letters A and H. I suspect that represents Adolf Hitler. Try that as the password."

Emma turned back to her keyboard, searched the file, and initiated opening it, typing in Adolf Hitler to the password box. The file correctly responded. Emm shouted, "That worked! You are so smart."

Emma, knowing fluent German, began reading the file silently. Emm spoke, "This is it. This file outlines the bank's involvement with the Nazis during the war and post-war."

After completing her reading for another thirty minutes, she turned to Jordan and summarized the critical tenants of the file. "Basically, this tells us that at the end of the war, the bank, and the Müller's worked to transport stolen art and other valuables out of Germany for the Nazis."

She added, "They first transported items to a collective location in Cologne, Germany, hiding it in a secret room in the basement of the Cologne Cathedral." [54]

Jordan asked, "Why there?"

Emm added, "The city of Cologne is on the Rhine River, providing access downriver to Basel, Switzerland. There was also a Gestapo headquarters in Cologne, which provided extra security. They selected the cathedral because the Allied bombing raids on the city mostly spared it."

Emm paused and then continued, "It says that they knew that the Cathedral, the largest Gothic church in Northern Europe, and second-tallest twin spires, would continue to be spared by the Allies. The Gestapo headquarters building was on Appellhofplatz, a few blocks from the Cathedral, making it easy to secure the church."

Again, Emm looked at Jordan, who was intently listening. She continued, "The three Gestapo leaders, Emanuel Schäfer, Franz Sprinz, and Kurt Matschke, encountered resistance to using the Cathedral from the local Roman Catholic Archbishop, Josef Frings. This obstruction only slightly deterred them. They seized control of the Cathedral in the summer of 1944. [55]

It goes on to say that they organized deliveries of truckloads of art and valuables. They stored the items in the basement, ideally protected from Allied bombing."

Jordan interrupted, "This is fascinating. What else does it say?"

Emm continued, "It states that the Germans knew the allies would be approaching by fall, knowing they had landed in Normandy in August and were advancing towards the Rhine River.

In November, the Germans controlled Aachen and the Colmar region, which still gave them control of the Rhine River to Switzerland. In mid-November, they emptied the hidden treasure room, putting it on barges and taking it downriver to Basel, Switzerland. [56]

They transported the stash to a bank branch and stored it in its vault."

Jordan asked, "Does it tell you anything about the type of valuables?"

Emm replied, "Yes, there is a list of art, jewelry, and other items." Emm read off some of the art listed.

Meanwhile, Jordan googled art stolen by Nazis. He cross-referenced it with the list Emm read, stating, "Emm, a website showing the ten most important masterpieces lost during World War II displays some of the art you are reading about."

He paused briefly, reading the list, assuredly saying, "It looks like seven of the ten items listed are on your list:
Raphael, *Portrait of a Young Man*
Vincent van Gogh, *Painter on His Way to Work*
Giovanni Bellini, *Madonna with Child*
Gustav Klimt, *Portrait of Trude Steiner*
Rembrandt van Rijn, *An Angel with Titus' Features*
Canaletto, *Piazza Santa Margherita*
Edgar Degas, *Five Dancing Women (Ballerinas)*" [57]

Emm added, "Also, there is a peculiar paragraph that seems like a cryptic instruction." She recited it to Jordan, "The German people present a singular mission unlike the two-faced duality of other nations; the mystical power of the Reich will unify our country, bringing order in the universe."

Jordan inquired, "So, what do we do now?"

Emm replied, "We should go to Basel and contact Interpol. Hopefully, they can meet us in Basel and acquire access to the bank vault."

Jordan jokingly asked, "Is there any chance we can go to Cologne? That is the home of true Kölsch beer. I'm dying to have one there."

Emm retorted, "Smartass!"

She quickly replied, "Perhaps a brief stopover in Cologne would be fun; let's get train tickets there and onward to Basel. We can have dinner in Cologne, have a Kölsch beer, and visit the cathedral. Seeing the cathedral and speaking with the head priest there might be worthwhile. We will need a hotel there and then to Basel the next day."

She shut down her computer, called Interpol, briefed the detective, and packed her clothes.

Meanwhile, Jordan made online train reservations for the next day to Cologne and the following day to Basel. He also secured lodging in both cities.

CHAPTER FOURTEEN
The Instruction

Josef entered Peter Müller's office in a bit of a panic. He urgently said, "Peter, I must interrupt and speak to you immediately."

Sitting behind his sizeable black forest wooden desk and speaking on a Zoom call, Peter said to the other participants, "Apparently, something requires my immediate attention. I need to log off this call. We can reschedule for tomorrow."

He turned his attention to Josef. "What is so urgent?"

Having already locked the door, Josef approached the desk, sitting in one of the two chairs facing it. He directly said, "We have had a system security breach."

Peter interjected, "How bad, and what did they get?"

Josef noted, "The breach pierced our firewall and targeted your files. The perpetrator stole no customer data and did not take any files."

Peter said, perplexed, "If they took nothing, then what is the problem?"

Josef, with trepidation, said, "It appears that the perpetrator breached the file labeled Neun."

Peter, now very disturbed, asked, "Any idea who?"

Josef replied, "We think it was the American, your new relative."

Peter turned his attention to the desk phone and removed the receiver from its cradle. He dialed a number, waiting for an answer.

Upon hearing a voice on the other end, he said, "I have a job for you. You are to follow the two Americans from yesterday's meeting. They are staying at the Bayerischer Hof Hotel. Keep me informed of their activity and wait for my instructions."

Peter looked at Josef and said, "It is being handled."

CHAPTER FIFTEEN
Next Stop Cologne

Emma and Jordan took a ten-minute taxi to the nearby Munich railway station the following morning. They boarded the DB Fernverkehr AG ICE 610 train, which departed at 9:27 am. It would be a four-hour and thirty-seven-minute direct train to Cologne.

A German private company operates the train across Germany and throughout Europe. This specific train is an intercity express. The ICE trains have first and second-class cars. All cars are air-conditioned, and the seating is the fundamental difference between the two classes.

First-class compartments usually have a seating configuration of two plus-one seats across the car, and second-class cars typically have a two plus-two seating across the vehicle.

Jordan booked the first-class car with two adjacent seats. This selection would also offer them extra legroom, meal service, access to a restaurant and lounge, and Wi-Fi service.

Once underway, Jordan and Emma relaxed in their seats, sipping coffee and eating the chocolate croissants they requested from the onboard cafe. They discussed their plans for arrival in Cologne sometime around 2:04 pm.

Emma commented, "When we arrive, we should take our bags to the hotel, leaving them with the bellman if we cannot secure our room. That way, we can get over to the Cathedral in the late afternoon before closing and then later freshen up and go to dinner."

Jordan replied, "That should easily work. I booked a deluxe double room at the Wyndham, directly across the street from the central railway station. The Breslauer Platz roundabout is the hotel's location. It is quite an easily recognized location.

The *Obelisk of Tutankhamun* by American artist Rita McBride adorns the center. From there, we can double back by taxi to the Cathedral, only a few blocks south of the railway station." [58]

He paused and continued, "After we visit the cathedral, we would walk a few blocks south toward the Rhine River to Peters Brauhaus, where we can get some authentic Kölsch beer." [59]

Emma smiled. "You have planned this through really well."

Jordan added, "Did you know that many of the Cologne pubs associate themselves exclusively with only one Kölsch beer brewery?"

Emma giggled, "No, I did not know that, but I am not surprised you know that."

"Indeed, Peters Brauhaus only offers its brewed Kölsch beer, so if we want to taste another one, we must move to another pub."

Emm smiled gleefully. "I get it."

They both relaxed comfortably in their seats for the duration of the ride. The train's speed made it somewhat challenging to fully grasp the passing scenery. Still, they could see changes in the topography.

The train route took them north of Basel to Cologne on the Rhine River. Cologne is nearly 300 miles northwest of

Munich and almost 300 miles north of Basel along the Rhine River.

The train traveled west across Germany to Stuttgart, revealing beautiful hillsides and luscious valleys. Many large deciduous and pine trees dot the landscape.

After leaving Stuttgart nearly halfway, they traveled north to Frankfort. The train moved west to Mainz and northwest along the Rhine River to Cologne.

The route along the Rhine River placed them in the Rhine Valley, where the landscape offered occasional vineyards and other farmland views.

Along the way, Emma occasionally daydreamed about the possible changes she could make when awarded the very beneficial financial inheritance. Would she and Jordan maintain their careers and stay in Annapolis? Would they get a bigger house? Most importantly, would they finally start a family?

Considering the extent to which Peter Müller and the Müller family potentially are involved in past and current support of the Nazi cause, she pondered her grandfather's role. She believed her grandfather had been a soldier of the Nazi party.

But she knew family, philanthropy, and community support defined his life, all while demonstrating American values.

Finding this treasure is essential to restoring her grandfather's reputation.

Lost in her thoughts, Emma did not realize they were pulling into the Cologne central station. The train was arriving on time.

Jordan interrupted her daydream. "Emma, we are pulling into the station. It is time to get our luggage and depart." They grabbed their luggage from the overhead storage and departed the train. They quickly found their way outside.

Neither Emma nor Jordan observed the two large men dressed in dark clothing exiting the train and following them.

They walked the short distance to the Wyndham Hotel on Breslauer Platz. The clerk informed them their room was not ready, but they could store their bags.

After leaving their bags with the hotel bellman for storage, they exited and quickly found a taxi to the Cathedral. It was only a short five-minute ride.

The Cologne Cathedral was a beautiful, enormous Gothic structure. The builders laid it out in the design of a Latin cross. Construction on the building started in 1248. It measured nearly 475 feet long and 283 feet wide, with over 85,000 square feet.

The towering 517-foot spires that reached far into the sky stood at the main entrance on the structure's west side. Medieval flying buttresses and pinnacles accented the east side of the structure. Eleven bells held positions throughout the structure.

Inside, the architecture was as stunning as the exterior. The massiveness of the structure was overwhelming, and the beauty drew one in as if being sucked into a monumental cavern.

The nave was 148 feet wide and reached nearly 200 feet high at the roof's ridge. There were stained glass windows lining each exterior wall. Each window looked to be over thirty feet tall and almost ten feet wide.

A set of five on the south side, called *Bayernfenster*, were a gift from Ludwig I of Bavaria and strongly represented the painterly German style of the time.

They walked through the cathedral. Their attention diverted to the multiple religious statues lining the walls and alcoves.

One particular treasure near the sacristy was the tenth-century *Crucifix of Bishop Gero*, the oldest known large crucifix, carved in oak with traces of paint and gilding. Additional treasures included the medieval stone statue of *St. Christopher*, looking down from the choir, and the *Dombild Altarpiece of the Three Kings*.

In the Sacrament Chapel rested the *Mailänder Madonna* ("Milan Madonna"), a High Gothic carving depicting the *Blessed Virgin and the Infant Jesus*. [60]

The most cherished antiquity in the cathedral was the *Shrine of the Three Kings*, completed sometime before 1200. Believed to be entombed in the shrine are the remains of the Three Wise Men, which is a large reliquary shaped like a basilica church made of bronze and silver, gilded and ornamented with fine details, figurative sculpture, enamels, and gemstones. [61]

After they walked through the entire inner circumference, observing all the religious artifacts, they walked back towards the entrance. Against the wall stood a traditional black, wrought iron candle station with purple glass candles and a money box for prayer offerings. They exited, noticing a gift shop building at the southeast corner of the cathedral.

The gift shop displayed various religious items, including books, rosaries, cathedral structures, religious statues, and imitation gold shrines for sale. They approached the women stationed at the checkout counter. In German, Emma asked, "Do you know if it would be possible to speak with one of the priests assigned to the cathedral?"

"For what purpose?" she replied.

"We are Americans with some questions about the cathedral during WWII. We were hoping a priest could provide us with some information," she replied.

"Let me check," she said as she lifted the phone and placed a call.

Emma listened in, overhearing the women confirm the priest's availability before she turned to tell Emma.

The woman stated, "Father Johann will be able to meet with you. He is on his way now."

Father Johann arrived, greeting both Emma and Jordan in English. He was a tall, handsome man, looking to be in his mid-forties. Unlike many priests who wore the traditional black floor-length cassock, he wore a black suit jacket and pants, a black shirt, and a Roman white collar.

After greeting them, he stated, "I understand you have some questions about the cathedral during WWII."

Jordan answered, "Yes, we are primarily interested in storing art and valuables by the Gestapo in late 1944."

Emma then filled in more information about her grandfather's story, their journey to Munich, their discovery of valuables stored in the cathedral, and their subsequent transport to Basel.

Father Johann said, "I think I may be of some assistance. Please, follow me." He led them outside the gift shop, around the cathedral, to another building at the northeast corner of the cathedral.

"This building is a small cathedral museum with additional artifact displays. Its primary floor contains pictures of various historical construction stages, key parish figures, and events. The museum building houses multiple offices on the second floor."

Father Johann added, "As a priest on staff at the cathedral, the administration assigned an office to me. My primary duty is managing this museum in addition to my traditional mass and parish duties." He led them into his office and continued, "Please take a seat. I need to retrieve a few old files and will return shortly."

Emma and Jordan sat patiently in the small, sparse office. It contained a desk, a bookshelf, and a small circular table with four armchairs, two of which they now occupied. Within approximately fifteen minutes, Father Johann returned carrying a handful of files. Sitting them on the table, he stated, "I think these will help answer some of your questions." He sat in one of the remaining vacant chairs.

Jordan asked, "What are these?"

Father Johann proudly explained, "These are files from the WWII period. Many of them contain written notes by Cardinal Josef Frings. He served as Archbishop of Cologne from 1942 until retirement in 1969. He vehemently opposed Hitler and Nazism."

Emma said, "Thank you."

Father Johann stated, "I will leave you both to review these files. I will attend to my other work and return in about one hour to answer any questions."

Emma and Jordan each grabbed a file and evaluated it for information. Each time Jordan encountered a German-language document, he extended it to Emma to translate. They had nearly completed their review of all files when Father Johann returned. He asked, "Have you found these files to be helpful?"

Emma boldly stated, "We certainly have. They provide quite a bit of information and context in our quest. I want to summarize our findings to ensure we have interpreted them correctly."

Father Johann replied, "Certainly, I am familiar with these files, but it has been a while since I reviewed them."

Emma summarized, "According to Cardinal Frings, his good friend, Father Otto Müller, died in a Berlin police hospital in October 1944." He had been active in the Resistance movement, arrested following the July plot of Operation Valkyrie to assassinate Hitler, and tortured by the Gestapo before being moved to the police hospital where he died. [62]

This event coincides with three Gestapo leaders— Emanuel Schäfer, Franz Sprinz, and Kurt Matchke—coming to the Cardinal to commandeer the use of the cathedral basement to store valuables that summer. The Cardinal feared that his further obstruction might lead to a similar outcome as his priest friend, so he relinquished the cathedral to the Gestapo."

She paused and added, "The Cardinal tells us there were indeed truckloads of valuables delivered to the cathedral and stored in the basement. It describes the valuables as works of art, statues, jewelry, watches, china, crystal, silverware, and others. The cathedral withstood fourteen hits by aerial bombings, according to his account. He also confirms the movement of the entire treasure trove to barges in November 1944 and transported down the Rhine River. But He did mention that he did not know the destination."

Jordan, giving Emma time to rest verbally, continued, "The files also tell us that on March 6, 1945, the American 3rd Armored Division entered Cologne, encountering a German division of Panzer tanks. A nearby Panzer tank destroyed two Sherman tanks before being knocked out by an American Pershing tank. The annihilated Panzer remained outside the cathedral until the war ended." [63]

Jordan paused and continued, "Repairs to the Cathedral started immediately following the war, lasting until 1956. As part of the reconstruction process, Otto Doppelfeld led an investigation into the basement and foundation to investigate potential damage to the foundation. He found evidence of valuables stored in the basement, primarily by recovering some incidental jewelry and chinaware. His excavation also revealed previously unknown details of earlier buildings on the site." [64]

Emma asked Father Johann, "Are we correct in understanding the information in these files?"

He replied, "Yes, you have accurately translated the information."

Jordan interjected, "Well, at least this confirms they stored valuables here in the cathedral and transported them by barge on the Rhine River. It gives us confidence that they could have taken the valuables to Basel and perhaps stored them in a bank vault there."

Emma turned to Father Johann. "Thank you so much for your assistance. I think we should be leaving now."

"You are most welcome. I am happy I could help. Please get in touch with me if you need anything further," the priest said as he handed her his card.

Emma and Jordan exited the museum building. Jordan pointed across the street, "Emm, look! There's one brewpub that I want us to visit. It is Gaffel am Dom, serving Gaffel Kölsch beer." [65]

They crossed the street to an old building updated with a more contemporary décor. They headed straight to the very long bar, stretching the entire inside distance. Once there, they asked the bartender for one beer each.

Emma asked the bartender, "What is so special about Kölsch beer?"

The bartender explained, "Cologne, or Köln, as we Germans say, is the official home of Kölsch beer. Technically, we are the only place to call a beer a Kölsch. The EU sanctions this. Many countries, such as the United States, often violate these requirements. We brew our Kölsch beer under the strictest German Purity Law of 1516. [66]

Also, the beer is a light golden color, brightly fermented, and strongly hoppy. It is to be served in a 200-milliliter-tall Stange, or rod glass."

"Thank you. I am now educated on Kölsch beer." Emma clinked her glass with Jordan's, and they each drank their cold, crisp beer.

The bartender added, "I should also inform you that only eleven breweries currently operating near Cologne are authorized to brew true Kölsch beer."

Jordan stated, "I know that. I have picked three for us to try at three different brauhaus locations. Those are Gaffel, Früh, and Peters."

The bartender replied, "Those are all good. Früh is one of the city's originals, and the Becker Brothers started our Gaffel Kölsch in 1908. It is unique because it uses ale yeast layered in cold cellars."

Emma asked, "What about Peters Kölsch?"

The bartender replied, "It is a good Kölsch, made especially for their brauhaus. Frankly, their ambiance and food are the big attractions."

Emma admired the stange with the blue oval label outlined in silver and white letters reading Gaffel. She tilted back her glass, consuming the remaining liquid.

Jordan did similarly, commented, "This has a fairly fruity taste with a crisp hop finish."

He then paid for their drinks, and they exited the building.

Outside, Jordan said, "Okay, we now need to walk about two blocks on the other side of the Cathedral to Am Hof, and there we should find Brauhaus Früh am Dom. They serve Früh Kölsch." [67]

As they walked, Emma thought it was nice to break away from their quest and allow time to do something enjoyable. She realized how much this pleased Jordan.

She also mentally noted how wonderful the early evening weather suited her. It was still daylight, with a nice warm summer breeze.

They quickly found Früh am Dom, entering the brauhaus with its old-world décor. They immediately approached the nearby bar, behind which was an expansive array of tables and chairs to accommodate many patrons. Their plan was to have a Kölsch and then journey to Peters Brauhaus for dinner.

They ordered two Früh Kölsch, served in traditional stanges. This time, the glasses displayed the Früh insignia: an oval insignia, the top third in red and the bottom two-thirds in white, with red letters reading 'Früh.'

Jordan commented, "This one has a beautiful straw gold color and a big white head." After tasting it, he stated, "It has a citrus taste as well as both grass and slate."

Emm grinned. "Your description is so exact. I love seeing you enjoy this."

They drank their beverages, staying a mere twenty minutes before continuing their pub crawl and onwards Peters Brauhaus, their final location for the evening.

They walked one block south to Muhlengasse, then turned east towards the river to walk two blocks to the brauhaus. This street was closed to traffic, allowing only pedestrians.

Paved with gray square stones outlined in red brick, creating rather large square patterns for the street. Stone rectangles and free-standing concrete drum planters lined the streets, all with luscious green and well-manicured boxwood.

The brauhaus was on the left side, housed in a beautiful three-story white stone block-walled building. The top two floors appeared residential, with the ground floor accommodating the brauhaus.

Large bronze block letters anchored into the building regally proclaimed- Peters Brauhaus. A stately blue metal horizontal arch awning with white letters spelling "Peters Brauhaus" adorned the entrance. Mounted to its top was the Peters insignia. Two wall lanterns bracketed the entrance.

Once inside, they quickly observed that this was an even more old-world décor than the prior establishment. The floors were light-colored wood planks, showing many years of foot traffic.

The walls had dark wood paneling, extending about two-thirds from the floor towards the ceiling. Above that, they painted the plaster wall a light yellow, and just above the wood paneling was a one-row wall trim of white porcelain square trim with a blue pattern.

Multiple sections divided the brauhaus: a bar/brewery room and four smaller pub-like-sitting areas with tables, chairs, and high-top standing tables. Each table had a round, light-colored wood top on a single dark wood leg, with a circular brass ring near the bottom serving as a footrest.

A large main room, the braustube, attracted much attention. The ceiling provided its primary architectural display. It was a large, vaulted, oval-shaped stained-glass dome that extended the room's length and width.

The second floor shielded the dome, preventing it from reflecting natural light. Instead, there was electric lighting above the dome, which created a beautiful, colorful glow.

The window contained a black iron grid support system with many square panels of light-yellow glass. Accented with various red, blue, and green colors, were yellow squares, creating an almost vine-like border pattern. This same pattern stretched down the middle length of the dome.

Community tables filled the room, seating six to twelve patrons. Most tables had single chairs on each side, whereas the tables around the walls had bench seating with red cushions and single dark chairs on the opposite side.

They could smell the sweet aroma of the beer and the sumptuous flavors of the various German cuisines.

They asked to be seated in the braustube, requesting one table beside the wall. Emma sat on the bench, and Jordan sat opposite in the single chair. Many patrons sat, and the chatter of voices quickly filled the room.

They had not noticed the traditional beer serving method in these restaurants at their previous two stops because they sat at the bar. In each room, they could see servers moving through the room carrying a carousel tray of beer.

Each tray was round, holding exactly twelve Stange Kölsch; the only open spots were from those already served. These trays were either tin or white plastic, and each displayed the block Peters Brauhaus lettering.

A server approached them and asked, "Would you like a Kölsch?"

Jordan replied, "Yes, two, please."

The server laid two cardboard coasters containing the Peters insignia on their table, placing two stanges on them.

The atmosphere enveloped Emma and Jordan. They lifted their glasses and sipped their beverages. As thirsty as they were, they went from sipping to downing the Kölsch and summoned another tray-carrying server for a second.

The server stood at the table and delivered two additional stanges, placing each on the cardboard coasters. This time, the server used a pen to make a small slash mark on each coaster.

Emma asked, "Why are you doing that?"

The server responded, "That is how we track the number of Kölsch each person drinks."

Emma chuckled, "That is so clever." She then raised the stange to eye level, observing that this one displayed the Peters insignia.

It was a white and gray checkered square with an oval laid over the top. A band of red with gold letters outlined the oval. Inside the oval, the top portion showed a red brewhouse and underneath a broad white band with red Peters Brauhaus letters.

Like the others, she noticed that this beer had a crystal-clear gold body that allowed light to sparkle. The gold color rested below an inch of bright white foam. It smelled of apples and other fruits.

Jordan sipped his Kölsch, "This one taste similar but slightly different from the other two places. It has a bready malt flavor, some fruitiness, a bit more spicy hops, yet still quite crisp."

Just then, the waiter arrived, asking for their order.

Jordan ordered for them, "Emm will have the potato soup with smoked bacon to start, and the Peters beer beef in a spicy dark Peters Kölsch sauce with fresh red cabbage and dumplings.

I will have the sauerkraut soup with pork sausage to start and the Peters Brauhaus plate with two small pork schnitzel, along with fried bacon, potatoes, and salad. We will share a freshly baked apple strudel with vanilla ice cream and whipped cream for dessert."

Over the next hour and a half, they consumed their dinner and marked seven Kölsch each on their cardboard coasters. By the time they exited, night had fallen, and overhead lamps and store windows illuminated the streets.

Emma and Jordan walked through the old town district. Along their way, they passed the Rathaus City Hall and reading a plaque stating that on June 23, 1963, President John F. Kennedy gave a speech after signing the city's Golden Book. The speech commended German Chancellor Adenauer for his continued support of Western efforts for freedom and peace.

After walking a short distance to the Rhine River, they stood at the concrete embankment, admiring the lighted bridge, the half-dozen docked riverboats, and the many people casually heading to their evening activities.

They joined hands, walking a few blocks back to the Cathedral, which appeared stunning at night, lit by many ground levels and strategically located building lights.

The twin spires, each strikingly ominous, reached into the black sky, visible only because of the illumination of the lighting.

After one last walk around the Cathedral to the north side, they made their last walk a few blocks to the hotel, planning to sleep for the night, allowing rest for departure on an early train the following day to Basel. [68]

The one thing they never noticed all night was the two hulking, muscular men following them.

CHAPTER SIXTEEN
And the Next Stop is Basel

After a nearly five-hour train ride on the DB Fernverkehr AG, ICE 107 from Cologne to Basel, Switzerland, Emma and Jordan arrived at the Bahnhof Basel SBB station. They exited the station and found the bus for a short five-minute ride to the bus stop beside the Hilton Hotel on the corner of Aeschengraben and Nauenstrasse.

The Hilton Hotel was a five-star, six-story, glass modern structure across the street from De-Wette Park. They did not observe the two statuesque men in dark clothing departing the train.

The two men remained at an adequate distance to avoid being easily detected. Yet, they kept a keen eye on Jordan and Emma.

When they checked in, it was nearly 5:00 pm. Jordan told Emm, "Let's shower and get dressed for dinner. I have made reservations for us at one of the nicest Swiss cuisine restaurants in Basel."

It was a beautiful, warm evening. Emma and Jordan had plenty of time before dinner, so they took their time to enjoy the evening and each other's company as they walked the twenty minutes to Basel Minster, the Gothic twin-spire church at the old town square. [69]

Emma made a darting move towards the second abductor. He countered by pushing her with his left arm. This arm motion was the moment that Jordan had expected.

Knowing that the man was holding him with only one arm, quickly twisted his body, making his right shoulder perpendicular to the man's chest. Jordan intended to imitate a fireman's carry wrestling move.

He grabbed the assailant's right triceps with his left hand. He simultaneously dropped to his right knee, pulling the man's torso onto his shoulders.

Jordan quickly reached through the man's legs, grabbing his left upper thigh with his right hand. He now had complete control over the man's body.

Jordan then dropped his second knee and quickly tilted his left shoulder toward the ground. This action created a strong momentum that tumbled the man over Jordan, falling with a crash on his back.

Jordan also added his shoulder weight into the man's abdomen, which created the effect of knocking the wind out of him. He successfully flipped the man to the ground, pinning him there.

Emma rushed to the two men on the ground, applying a carotid control/vascular neck restraint, placing pressure on both sides of the man's neck, rendering him temporarily unconscious.

They quickly jumped up and raced through the park to the hotel across the street. The concierge immediately called the nearby Bahnhof Basel SBB police station.

The police arrived quickly, apprehending the two assailants, who were still unconscious.

One of their detectives interviewed Jordan and Emma in the hotel lobby. They explained who the men were, who they worked for, and why the attack occurred.

They also told the detective about their planned meeting with Interpol the next day and their intended visit to the bank. The detective replied that he would report tonight's attack to Interpol.

Jordan and Emm retired to the sanctuary of their room.

Both were messy and sweaty from their encounter, so they showered.

Emm was already in the shower and surprised when Jordan stepped in with her. His adrenaline, still pulsating, wanted to direct his affection and intensity towards Emma.

Emm, astounded, said, "This is a welcome surprise."

Jordan closed the shower door and reached out with both hands, grasping both of her breasts. They were large enough to fit within each hand's entire palm.

He wrapped his arms around her back, caressing downward across her lordosis to her buttocks, grabbing each cheek tightly, pulling her close to him.

She could feel his strong erection against her pelvis.

She kissed him as she applied bath gel to his body, providing a good lather for both. Once they rinsed, they quickly exited, and still wet, they fell into bed.

The shower foreplay had excited both their bodies, quickly allowing Jordan to penetrate. He and Emm moved rhythmically for nearly a minute.

Jordan could still smell the lavender shampoo in her hair.

He felt her abdomen and thigh muscles tighten and her breathing getting stronger.

He could feel her hands clasping at his shoulder blades and her thighs drawing against his legs.

Suddenly, she breathed intense relief into her body.

Emm was never a loud love maker; she allowed her body to release upon achieving her orgasm. Jordan experienced his release shortly after Emm.

He rolled off her. They both simultaneously said, "That was fun."

They snuggled for a while, satisfied to be in one another's embrace.

They fell asleep, thinking about their meeting with Interpol the next day.

CHAPTER EIGHTEEN
The Bank Vault

Jordan and Emma woke early the following day, having breakfast served in their room. They shared a pot of fresh Swiss mountain coffee, toasted English muffins, butter, and Swiss Alpine flower honey handcrafted from small bee colonies in the Bernese Mountains in Switzerland.

Fresh raspberries, blackberries, yogurt, and granola for Emma accompanied the other breakfast items. Jordan devoured a three-egg omelet with locally produced Swiss cheese and bacon.

After breakfast, they showered without the foreplay of the previous night and dressed for their meeting with Interpol Inspector Gaudot. Their mutual attire for the day was casual.

Jordan wore Levi's denim jeans, a heather heritage blue Travis Matthew golf shirt, and his Asics shoes. Emma wore designer jeans, an LL Bean pale rose Pima cotton short-sleeve crew-neck tee, and her Asics shoes. They certainly wanted to be on time.

They exited the elevator, stepping directly into the hotel lobby. A group of gentlemen, two dressed in dark-colored suits and three wearing police uniforms, stood in the center of the lobby. They approached, and Jordan asked, "Are one of you Inspector Gaudot?"

The taller of the two suit-wearing men reached out his hand. "Yes, I am Inspector Gaudot. May I assume you are the Murrays?"

Jordan reached out his hand. "I'm Jordan, and this is Emma."

Gaudot added, "As you may be aware, Interpol has no local jurisdiction in criminal matters. I took the liberty of contacting the local Basel police. I want to introduce Detective Brewer. These other three men are officers in his department."

Brewer reached out his hand. "Nice to meet the both of you."

Emma asked, "Will we be able to inspect the bank vault today?"

Brewer replied, "Certainly. I have secured the proper warrant."

The group proceeded outside, deploying into three awaiting Tesla police vehicles. The short ten-minute ride down the hill to the bank building on the corner of Freie Street and Street. Alban-Graben was uneventful.

Brewer led the group entering the bank. The lobby was a typical cavernous structure with white and black porcelain floor tile and white painted walls ordained with various watercolor paintings of Swiss scenes.

He hurried to the security guard sitting behind a large countertop desk. He conversed with the seated security guard. The guard wore police-type clothing with various essential security gears but no gun. He was a middle-aged man, somewhat portly, with dark hair.

The guard made a phone call, asking him to wait.

Within five minutes, an attractive middle-aged woman in a gray skirt business suit approached, asked, "I am Sophie Favre, Vice President of Bank Operation. I understand you have a warrant to search our vault. May I see the warrant?"

"Certainly," Brewer said, handing her the warrant. He gazes at her attractive legs and feminine features, concluding she would be worthy of asking out on a date, but that would be for another time.

She read the warrant while walking over to the security desk. She made a phone call. They heard her telling someone about the warrant.

Sophie returned smugly, stating, "I am authorized to assist you. I will escort you to our vault, located two subfloors below. Please follow me."

The group split up and rode two elevator loads to reach the entrance to the vault room.

Sophie punched the numerical code into the vault's keypad and placed her eyes on the adjacent retinal scan. The heavy concrete door with steel cladding slowly moved open.

Emma waited impatiently, anxiously anticipating what might lie behind the door. Jordan, also excited, grasped Emma's hand. The police professionals showed no emotion, simply waiting patiently to search.

Once the door was wide open, the team entered. Much to the team's surprise, there was frankly nothing noticeable there. The vault room was rather stark.

On one expansive wall, there stood a bank of safety deposit boxes. In the center, there stood a lightly stained wooden table with eight armed wooden chairs matching the table's-stained color. The floor had stamped concrete with a slightly green tint color added.

On a second wall, there was a series of what appeared to be large lockers. On the wall opposite the safety deposit boxes was a blank wall with several old pictures and bank memorabilia.

One photo showed the original bank name, Munich German Bank, Basel Switzerland branch, 1935. To its side hung a picture of the bank executives with names, and one could identify the original bank president, Fritz Müller, Henry's father.

On the fourth wall stood three additional smaller vault doors, each with its keypad for entry.

Emma commented, "There does not appear to be anything here."

Sophie Favre responded, "I could have told you that you would not find any stored Nazi treasure here. We are a reputable bank. Our depositors know and trust us to maintain their valuables discretely and ethically."

Inspector Gaudot interjected, "Yes, but perhaps there are individual items stored in some of these boxes and lockers whose exact contents you do not know."

Jordan added, "And what about these three other vault doors?"

Sophie replied, "Those are private vaults. Two belong to local businessmen, and the one in the middle belongs to our current bank CEO, Peter Müller."

Jordan looked at Emma and said, "They must be hiding the treasure in the vault." He looked at Detective Brewer and asked, "Does the warrant extend to everything inside this main vault, meaning the boxes, lockers, and these three vaults?"

"Well, yes, it certainly does," Brewer replies.

Inspector Gaudot turned to Sophie, pointed to the middle door, and asked, "Would you be so kind as to open this vault door for us?"

Sophie replied, "I can assist you with any box or vault except that one. Only Mr. Müller has the keypad code to that vault." She added, "He is unavailable today and we cannot reach him."

Jordan excitedly turned to Emma, asked, "Emm, what was that cryptic statement you discovered in that file?"

She pulled out her iPhone, looking for the note she had filed. She read it aloud:

"The German people present a singular mission unlike the two-faced duality of other nations; the mystical power of the Reich will unify our country, bringing order in the universe."

Jordan sat at the table, grabbed a piece of notepaper and pen, and asked Emma to repeat the statement while transcribing it to the paper. He quickly underlined specific words: duality, mystical, unity, and order.

He looked up, shouted, "I've got it!"

The team members all turned their eyes to Jordan, listening intently.

Holding the notepad, Jordan stood and stated, "There are cultural associations of numbers. The Pythagoreans, or Greeks, had a strong association with such. For instance, the number ten is associated with perfection. In Emm's statement, I have underlined four words, and I believe each is associated with a specific number." [71]

He paused, assuring that all were listening. He continued, "The word 'duality' is the number two, the word 'mystical' is the number three, the word 'unity' is the number one, and the word 'order' is the number four. Thus, the combination is 2314."

Detective Brewer walked to the middle vault door and punched the combination 2314. The keypad beeped, illuminating a green light, and the door latch triggered open. Brewer grabbed the handle, pulling it wide open for all to enter.

She paused and continued, "It also describes that a second boat, U-530, also journeyed through the Canary Islands picking up supplies, Nazis, and treasure with orders to proceed to Argentina, similarly expelling it human and material cargo, and then onward to Mar del Plata to surrender."

Jordan jumped in with additional information, "I just googled both U-977 and U-530, and while there is no confirmed documentation about Nazi passengers or treasure cargo, there is documentation that both U-boats traveled through the Canary Islands in the summer of 1945 to Argentina, and surrendered at Mar del Plata. The U-530 boat surrendered on July 10, 1945, and the U-977 boat surrendered on August 17, 1945." [81]

Both Emma and Jordan stopped summarizing their findings. Emma grinned at Jordan, said, "Well, how do you feel about one more junket in our quest?"

"You mean Argentina?" was his response.

"Yes," was all she said with confidence and a smile.

CHAPTER NINETEEN
Informing Hilda

Back in their hotel room, Emma called Hilda. She wanted to brief Hilda about their discoveries and alert her to the upcoming likely arrest of Peter Müller.

Emma placed the phone on the table and pressed the speaker button to ON. She wanted Jordan to hear the conversation.

"Hello," the voice on the other end announced. It was Hilda.

"Hilda, this is Emma and Jordan," Emma replied.

"Oh, so nice to hear from you," Hilda stated.

Emma said, "Hilda, I wanted you to know that your suspicion communicated to me at the restaurant was correct."

"Oh, what do you mean?" Hilda inquired.

Emma continued, "After you confided to me your concern, I accessed some bank files, specifically Peter's files, which incriminated him and the Müller family in long-standing support of the Nazis during WWII and for years afterward. We used that information to follow a trail to Cologne and Basel.

We enlisted the support of Interpol and the Basel police. In Basel, we gained access to a bank branch vault and then to a secret inner vault belonging to Peter. We discovered a trove of stolen Nazi art and other valuables."

Hilda was astounded. "Oh my stars, of course, I was concerned, but I never thought it would develop into something like this. I had no exact involvement."

Emma added, "Also, in Basel, two men attacked Jordan and me in a park there. They were the security men from the bank conference room that day we met in Munich."

Hilda asked, "Are you okay?"

"Yes, Jordan and I are both okay. We escaped successfully, render the two men incapacitated, and contact the local police to have them apprehended. I understand that they have confessed to being instructed by Peter to attack us."

"This is all so disturbing," Hilda inserted.

Emma professed, "I wanted you to know that Interpol and the local Munich German police will probably apprehend Peter within the next couple of days." She stopped and continued, "They probably will come to seek information from you, too."

"Of course, I will cooperate fully with them," she replied.

Hilda added, "Emma, you know the bank has always had a family member at the helm and on the board, at the very least. I am too old to be considered for such a role now. Considering your family ties, it would not surprise me if they named you to the board as the family representative."

Emma stated, "We can cross that bridge when we come to it. That is not a necessary decision for today."

Hilda responded, "I know this outcome is not what you ever intended when you set out to learn about Heinrich's family. I am very grateful that you have made this discovery, as painful as it is for the Müller family. I am certainly glad you are safe. Now what?"

Emma replied, "Jordan and I are going to travel to Argentina. There appears to be one additional element on which we must put a final touch."

"I wish you a continued safe journey and look forward to seeing you soon back in Munich," Hilda said.

"Thank you, and we will indeed return to Munich," Emma closed. She then pressed the red end call button on her phone.

Emma turned to Jordan and asked, "Have you arranged our trip to Argentina?"

"Not exactly," he replied.

Emma looked at him with a concerned expression and asked, "What does that mean?"

Jordan proudly stated, "I thought sailing from Gibraltar to the Canary Islands would be fun. It would be fun and allow us to visit the Villa Winter to determine if we can learn any additional facts there."

Emma looked at him, a bit surprised and silent.

Jordan continued, "You might recall that this was a bit of a bucket list thing we discussed at the Academy. I have already contacted Troy and asked him to join us. He is taking time off for this sailing trip and bringing his new girlfriend."

Emma stared at Jordan and said, "Well, I guess you have already made the decision." She paused and gleefully added, "I love the idea."

"Great," he declared. He added, "I've already reserved a boat, and we will fly from Basel to Gibraltar International Airport tomorrow."

CHAPTER TWENTY
Going to Gibraltar

Emm and Jordan found themselves early at the Basel airport the following morning. They were taking the British Airways flight 751, departing at 6:50 am to Gibraltar. The entire trip would be eight hours, twenty-five minutes, with one stop. The layover would be in London for three hours and fifty minutes.

Jordan had purchased two seats in the Club Europe front section of the plane. This trip allowed for seat choice, and he chose an aisle and window seat in row 2. These seats provided them with ample room compared to the standard seats in the plane's rear.

Jordan was getting accustomed to being able to afford the better seats for long flights.

After only one hour forty-five minutes of flight, they landed at London's Heathrow Airport Terminal 5. Their next flight to Gibraltar was departing from Terminal 3. They were not in any rush, as they would have a three-hour fifty-minute layover, with their flight leaving at 11:25 am. That flight would take two hours and fifty minutes.

After exiting the plane, they found the free London underground shuttle train available for inter-terminal transfers between Terminal 5 and Heathrow Terminal 2 & 3. It only took twenty minutes to arrive at Terminal 3.

Once inside Terminal 3, Emm looked at Jordan and said, "I sure would like something to eat. It will be a long while before we arrive in Gibraltar."

"I agree," replied Jordan. "Where would you like to eat?"

"Well, I am quite unfamiliar with this airport. Let's walk through the terminal, and we can choose something interesting."

They walked down the terminal concourse, passing several eating establishments and retail stores. They eventually came upon E L & N. After reading the menu in the window, Emma said, "This looks perfect." The hostess seated them. [82]

The waitress immediately greeted them and asked if she could bring them anything to drink. Emm ordered the Caffè latte, and Jordan ordered the macchiato. They both commented that they would need longer to review the menu for their food order.

Emm and Jordan exchanged commentary about the exciting menu choices and their descriptions. Jordan asked Emm, "What are you going to order?"

She replied, "I think I will order the smashed avocado toast. They serve that sandwich on thick sourdough with smashed avocado, fresh chili, coriander, and poached egg. I am going to add smoked salmon." She stopped, smiled at Jordan, and asked, "And you?"

"I am thinking about ordering eggs Benedict served in an English muffin, poached eggs, turkey bacon, hollandaise, avocado, and chili butter." He paused and added, "And I will order some truffle fries. Perhaps you would want to share?"

Emm replied, "Of course."

After about ten minutes, the waitress returned with their beverages. She asked, "Are you ready to order?"

Emm replied, "Yes, I will have the smashed avocado toast, and the smoked salmon."

The waitress turned to Jordan. He responded, "I will have the eggs benedict and a side order of truffle fries."

The waitress turned to leave, and Emm stopped her, wanting to add to her order. "I would also like to get a piece of the saffron dulce de leche." Jordan gasped, surprised at this dessert selection. He glanced at the menu and read, vanilla saffron sponge cake, cream, milk, and saffron.

He looked up gleefully, stating, "That looks delicious. Hopefully, you will share." Emm, laughing, said, "Of course, silly."

They ate their food and ordered another round of beverages. They needed to kill some more time. After exhausting almost two hours, they paid their bill and left the restaurant.

They wandered along the concourse until they found their departure gate. They would only need to sit for over an hour before boarding started.

The second leg of the flight would be on the British Airways A320, which has a different seating configuration. Preferred seating is the first ten rows, but they had three seats on each side. Jordan reserved row six, seats B and C, with an aisle for himself and the middle for Emm.

Once seated and the flight had taken off, Emm turned to Jordan and asked, "What type of sailboat did you rent?"

Jordan proudly expressed, "I rented a Lagoon 40. It's a catamaran instead of a monohull. With it being wider at over twenty-two feet, it will provide greater stability and room, especially since it has a larger kitchen and cooking area for four of us to be comfortable.

It has a large indoor salon area with a full kitchen, cabinet space for storage, and a collapsible table with comfortable sofa seating. The aft deck or outside salon is also quite inviting. It also has a nice table surrounded by comfortable sofa seating.

You step up to the cockpit, where the helm sits, along with all the radar and navigation instrumentation. The manufacturers designed the cockpit so one person could sail the boat. Still, since there will be four of us, working the sails, anchor, etcetera will be easy.

It has two forty-five-horsepower diesel engines with a fuel tank capacity of 106 gallons. The width allows for two trampolines at the bow, allowing ample sunbathing space. There is an inflatable dingy hoisted at the stern with a fifteen-horsepower engine. It will accommodate four people.

The solar panels will provide the power needed for electricity and a water purification system with a water tank capacity of seven-nine gallons. Being outfitted with a square top mainsail allows for increased speed and a self-tacking jib. There is also an optional code zero mainsail, which, when used, will add quite a bit of speed."

Emm intently listened and replied, "It sounds wonderful. And what about sleeping berths?"

Jordan told her, "The Lagoon 40 has three different sleeping configurations. Those are three cabins with two heads, four cabins with two heads, and four cabins with four heads. This model is the three cabins with two heads, often called an owner's version. This version is usually without a charter service.

The port side has a single cabin, head, and large dressing and storage area. We'll take the cabin.

The starboard side has two cabins, front and rear, with a shared head in the middle. Troy and his new girlfriend will share that side."

Emm inquisitively asked, "What do we know about this new girlfriend?"

Jordan replied, "Not much. She is Janessa and works in the administration department at the Hampton VA Medical Center near the university. Troy has been dating her for a little over a month. He seems very smitten with her."

"Well, we need to learn more about her when we meet her. This conversation should be quite interesting, given that in the past, Troy has never stayed in a relationship very long," she replied.

They both settled in for the rest of the flight. Jordan took a brief nap, and Emm read a few magazines she had picked up at the airport concourse.

CHAPTER TWENTY-ONE

Rendezvous with an Old Friend

Upon landing at the Gibraltar International Airport, they retrieved their luggage and proceeded outside to a very sunny late morning.

Jordan said he rented the sailboat from the Gibraltar boat rental in Marina Bay, near the famous Ocean Village. It is on the peninsula's western side and is a short walk from the airport.

They exited the small terminal and found their way to the crosswalk. Uniquely, this airport required pedestrians to cross the runway to get to the other side. A security gate blocked walkers while plans landed. The gate functioned like a drawbridge raised to block cars while boats moved through the open space.

The gate raised after almost thirty minutes, allowing them to proceed. The early morning heat had already caused them to sweat. They pulled their wheeled luggage for about fifteen minutes to reach the marina. It took another ten minutes to find the office of the boat rental company.

Jordan conversed with the office manager, signed the paperwork, and acquired the boat's keys. The manager informed him that the one-way rental would incur an extra fee.

The office manager escorted them to the slip where they docked the Lagoon 40. He gave them a walkthrough with various instructions regarding the boat's operation.

After the manager left, Emma and Jordan stowed their belongings in the portside cabin and organized their items for the trip. This cabin seemed voluminous compared to the two smaller cabins on the starboard side.

Troy and Janessa were due within the next hour, so they sat on the cushioned seats around the table on the aft outside salon.

Emm asked, "How many days will the trip take us?"

Jordan replied, "It is 630 nautical miles from Gibraltar to the Canary Islands. We should arrive in four to five days if we travel at five nautical miles an hour."

"Thanks. I need to start a list for provisions, and now I know for how long," Emm replied. "I will review my list with Troy and Janessa when they arrive. We can then go to the store to make purchases."

"Good idea," replied Jordan. "Add to your list purchasing a couple of good ice chests and the ice to store food. The refrigerator on this boat is quite small."

"Okay, and you should remember to purchase a couple of extra jerry cans to have extra diesel," she responded factually.

Jordan smiled and said, "Of course you are correct. Also, add some suntan lotion and other personal items, such as toothpaste, shaving cream, and any other items you chose."

A hearty voice interrupted the two as they continued to present items needed on the list.

"Ahoy, mate."

They both looked up, turning their heads towards the dock. Simultaneously, they saw Troy and a very stunning woman approaching. They waved, shouting, "Come aboard."

Jordan could not help but stare at Janessa. She was indeed a stunning woman. Janessa was slender, about five feet eight inches tall, with a well-shaped body, attractive long legs, dark hair, dark eyes, and a light brown skin tone. He immediately thought she looked like a young Halle Berry.

Troy and Janessa handed their luggage to Jordan, stepped on the starboard rear transom, and boarded the boat. Troy gave Jordan a quick salute. "Hello, captain."

Jordan returned the salute and said, "It's commander, remember?" They laughed and Jordan gave Troy a giant bear hug. "It's great to see you."

Meanwhile, Emma cordially greeted Janessa, "It is such a pleasure to meet you. We are so looking forward to getting to know you."

Janessa smiled and said, "I am also looking forward to getting to know Troy's two best friends. He has told me so much about you both."

"Well, we will have plenty of 'get-to-know-you time' for later. For now, we need to get you both situated below. Then we need to get to the store for provisions and other essentials for the trip."

"Sounds great," Janessa replied.

Emma responded, "By the way, are you familiar with sailing?"

"Not especially. I have been out a few times with Troy on his boat back in Virginia, but never anything for extended days."

"Well, you will have much to learn," replied Emma.

Emma and Jordan instructed them towards the starboard side cabins. They gave each other a smirk when they observed that Troy and Janessa were stowing their gear in an apparent effort to share a cabin.

After stowing their gear, Emma and Jordan gave the two newcomers a quick boat tour and general instructions. They agreed there would be more time to discuss details before sailing departure the following day. They needed to get provisions and essentials.

For efficiency, they split the duties of acquiring their provisions and essentials. Emma and Janessa agreed to do the grocery shopping. Emma had already reviewed the list with Janessa and Troy, who added some items. Jordan and Troy would get the ice chests and ice, as well as the jerry cans and diesel.

It took nearly two hours to gather all the items on the list before returning to the boat. It took another hour to get everything organized and stored. The ladies handled storing all the dry foods while the guys attended to properly packing the ice chests. One chest contained beef products and chicken, the second, fresh vegetables and fruit, and the third, the beverages.

The guys had taken the liberty of purchasing a mixed case of wine, six bottles of Spanish White Albariño, six bottles of Spanish Red Ribera del Duero Tempranillo, and two cases of a local craft beer. After storing their provisions, they all sat outside at the salon table with beverages. Jordan and Troy each had a cold Bushy's Gibraltar Barbary Beer. When poured into their glasses, the ale displayed a copper hue with a nice inch-thick mousse-like white foam head. It smelled of pleasant roasted bread. It tasted slightly bitter, with hops forward, balanced by malt, providing flavors of biscuit and caramel.

The girls each had a glass of refreshing cold Spanish Albariño white wine. It presented a light golden hue in their glasses. It tasted similar to a Chenin Blanc with flavors of lemon zest, grapefruit, honeydew, nectarines, and salt and ended with a slight bitterness.

Emma lobbed the first direct question to Janessa. "So, tell us about yourself and how did you two meet?"

"Well, I grew up near Pittsburgh, Pennsylvania, in a small town, Wexford, in the north hills area. I was a good academic high school student and a competitive cheerleader. Penn State University awarded me an academic scholarship. I tried out for the cheerleader squad and was fortunate to make it and cheer for all four years. After graduating from Penn State University, I attended the University of North Carolina, earning my Master of Health Administration. I worked at Atrium Health Carolinas Medical Center in Charlotte until two years ago, when I moved to Hampton for the position of AVP for the Hampton VA Medical Center," said Janessa.

Troy interjected, "That's where we met. I had to go to the VA hospital for a checkup, and we met there in the cafeteria line. The hospital is a short walk from campus."

Janessa continued, "I live fairly close to the hospital at the Roseland townhomes."

Again, Troy jumped in. "You two might remember those townhomes, as their parking lot borders the wall to the Hampton Phoebus National Cemetery."

Emma gasped out loud. "Oh, my goodness. What a coincidence."

Of course, Janessa was unaware of their nighttime exploit in the cemetery. Troy had yet to brief her on the entire story. He figured that would come out during their sailing cruise.

Janessa added, "Troy asked me out for dinner. I said yes. And we have been dating steadily for a little over a month. I was very excited when he invited me to join him and you both on this trip."

The foursome spent the next two hours continuing the question-and-answer game. Janessa also turned the tables on Emma and Jordan, asking questions of them.

After two hours, Troy changed the subject, asked Jordan about the voyage details, "So how long do you calculate the sail will take, and when do you want to depart?"

Jordan answered, "By my calculation, I estimate the trip to be 630 nautical miles, and traveling at five knots should take four to five days. Let's depart tomorrow at 9:45 am. That will be low tide, making it easier to get underway. If we wait until later in the day, we will encounter a high-water mark with the tide coming in, which will cause us to lose speed."

"That sounds logical," Troy said. "And where are we going to make port in the Canary Islands?"

"Our first port will be Lanzarote Marina on the closest island of Lanzarote. It is at the northern end of the chain of Canary Islands," Jordan stated.

After one day's rest, we will make a ten-hour sail to reach the southern end of the island of Fuerteventura. We will dock at the Puerto de Morro Jable Marina." [83]

"That's a lot of sailing," announced Janessa. "When do we do something other than sailing?"

"Good question," stated Jordan. "Once we dock in Fuerteventura, we will journey across the island by jeep to visit Villa Winter, sometimes called Casa Winter. That is our fundamental goal for this trip. It was a unique home and compound built during the WWII era for Germans by a German. We found some research information regarding the use of the villa by the Germans, and we want to inspect it ourselves."

Emma interjected, "I will fill you in on the entire story tomorrow when we are underway. It will make for a pleasant discussion while we are out in the open water. There are some details that Troy already knows, but I need to bring him up to speed as well."

Janessa eagerly replied, "I can't wait to hear this story."

Jordan continued, "After we visit the villa and perhaps spend an additional day relaxing, we will sail a little over one hundred nautical miles, taking about twenty-four hours to the island of Tenerife. That is where we will leave the boat and take flights from there."

Troy announced confidently, "Well, I made the same calculation as you, knowing about the first leg of this sailing adventure. While flying over, I prepared a chart with rotational assignments for each of us at the helm. I suggest we rotate in three-hour shifts between the four of us. I will train Janessa and watch her for her first couple of shifts. Also, I prepared work assignments for cooking, cleanup, etcetera."

"That's terrific, thank you," stated Emma.

Jordan concluded, "Well, we better get some sleep. We have a long day starting tomorrow."

The foursome gathered their garbage, locked the doors, stowed their gear for the night, and headed to their cabins.

CHAPTER TWENTY-TWO
Another Sailing Adventure

The following day, Janessa was the last to wake up. After brushing her teeth and a bit of morning prep, she slid back the door leading to the three small steps up to the salon.

Janessa wore tight khaki shorts and a teal-colored crew neck tee shirt, which fit well but did not fit tightly. Once there, she immediately met Jordan, who was cooking breakfast in the small rear corner kitchen. She could smell bacon and eggs. He also had heated bagels in a cooking pan since they had no toaster.

Music was playing. Jordan had his Pandora set to oldies rock and roll. Ironically, the song playing as she entered the salon was *"Long Cool Woman in a Black Dress"* by the Hollies.

"Good morning," said Janessa. "What time is it?"

"It is 7:13," said Jordan, being precise.

Janessa turned and saw Troy and Emma sitting outside the salon table. They were each holding a cup of coffee.

The salon door was already open. Janessa walked outside. "Good morning," she said to the two sitting comfortably.

They simultaneously said, "Good morning."

"I did not realize I would be the last one to awake," she added.

"No problem," said Troy. "I wanted to let you sleep. It might be less comfortable from here on out."

"Would you like some fresh coffee?" asked Emma.

"Most certainly," responded Janessa.

Janessa sat down beside Troy on the gray cushioned seating along the port side wall of the outside salon. Emma poured Janessa a cup of coffee and explained that a French press brewed the coffee as they had no coffee maker onboard or Keurig machine.

Jordan smelled the aroma of coffee wafting up to her nose on the morning breeze as it poured into her cup.

Jordan then brought a plate of scrambled eggs, bacon broiled in the oven with brown sugar and a slight bit of cayenne pepper and skillet-grilled everything: bagels, cream cheese on the side, and some fresh apple slices.

They each filled their plates. Janessa appreciated the eggs being soft and firm without being runny, and the bacon had an excellent sweet taste with a hint of spiciness that remained on her palate. The bagel tasted better than the traditional toaster method. Grilled bread on the inner side had a slight spread of butter, adding that flavor to the sprinkled everything mix on the outside, along with a nicely brown grilled coating on the inner side. The actual inside of the bagel remained soft. Adding the regular white cream cheese that melted on the warm bagel provided a terrific mouthful taste combination.

Jordan commented, "I thought we should have a huge breakfast today to get us started. I am not sure we will want to cook this way too many mornings."

Troy said, "Thanks, Jordan."

Emma asked, "What time do we need to get underway?"

"We should pull away from the dock around 9:30. That gives us about two hours to finish up breakfast, clean up, get organized, and go over a last review of everything," Jordan stated.

Troy announced, "Good. Per my rotation job chart, I will assume the first three-hour shift at the helm. The order will follow me: Emma, Jordan, and then Janessa." He paused and saw all heads nodding in agreement. "I changed this following our discussion last night because I was concerned that the original order had Janessa on one shift in the middle of the night. Of course, when Janessa takes her first shift, I will stay with her, instructing and observing."

Jordan proclaimed, "That will be very important. Based upon the new rotation, she will be on the shift from 6:30 pm to 9:30 pm and again from 6:30 am to 9:30 am. At both times, at least one of us will probably be awake with her. This way, she won't be on the dark hour rotation times."

Emma added, "Yes, at least to start; Jordan and I will have the shifts corresponding to the dark hours. We can always change that later in the trip if necessary and, as Janessa gains experience at the helm."

Once they had devoured their morning feast, Janessa volunteered to wash dishes and do general cleanup. This left the three sailing experts to do a final once-over review of all provisions and conditions on the boat, similar to an airline pilot conducting their checklist before takeoff. They stowed everything, and all reviews were completed by 9:00 am, giving the crewmates about thirty minutes of final relaxation time.

CHAPTER TWENTY-THREE
Orcas and Pirates

Troy, wearing a pair of Fair Harbor mist-colored swim shorts and a heather gray performance tee shirt, was at the helm when he issued his order to Jordan to cast off the bow portside line and simultaneously to Emma to release the aft portside line.

Troy wore a pair of Vuori stormy-colored Kore shorts and a light blue long-sleeved wind shirt to protect his skin from the sun better. Emma wore white micro-mesh shorts and a gray square-neck tank top. All four crew members wore hats and polarized sunglasses.

The boat was facing forward from its docking berth, making it easy to get underway. Troy had already started the engines, pushing the throttle forward and allowing thrust to move them away from the dock.

He guided the boat slowly out of the marina into open water. Janessa was already sitting in the collapsible cushioned seat on the bow deck in front of the salon windows. However, it still needs to be added to the trampoline netting. She had determined that the position would allow her to observe Emma and Jordan as they assisted with the sails. She was not yet wearing a swimsuit. Instead, she donned a comfortable pair of blue shorts and a white short-sleeve midriff shirt with a low scooped crew neck collar, allowing some respectable display of cleavage.

Once they were outside the confines of the marina, in open water, Troy gave the order to hoist the jib sail first and then the mainsail. The rigged boat left the helmsman able to do this alone, but there was no need with a crew of four. Once they fully deployed the sails, they immediately realized there was insufficient breeze to provide speed. After some conversation, the group agreed to motor sail until the breeze hopefully increased. With the engines on full throttle, a slight breeze in the sails, and an outgoing tide, they could achieve just fewer than five knots of speed.

The achieved boat speed provided barely enough momentum to combat the incoming current. The Atlantic current entered the Mediterranean Sea at four to six knots, creating a headwall difficult for a sailboat to counteract.

For the next three hours, the boat progressed without issue.

Troy asked Janessa to join him at the helm during his middle one hour. He instructed her to read the electronic navigation chart, explaining that it was much like driving a car. He said that the chart plotted a blue line, their intended course. She would need to steer the boat to stay on the blue line. He also explained that the radar plotted other boats and hazards in the area. She should watch that but also scan the area visually around her periodically.

Troy showed her how to throttle the engines and read the tell-tales on the sails for wind direction. Those are small pieces of fabric attached to the sail which will blow toward the wind. He attempted to show her how to trim the sails for such, but finally instructed her to call one of them when needed.

He reviewed emergency procedures at the helm and elsewhere on the boat, specifically pointing out the life preservers stored under one of the inside salon seating areas.

Troy instructed Janessa to retrieve one of the life preservers. He showed how to secure it effectively around her upper torso. After she felt fully versed in its use, she placed the life preserver on the outside salon seat.

After being briefed, Janessa joined Emma, lying on the trampoline at the front of the boat, relaxing before her shift in one hour. They both took advantage of the mid-morning sunshine, basking in its warmth.

Emma asked, "So, how do you now feel after your brief tutorial on sailing?"

"I feel confident and grateful you changed the rotation, as I was nervous about taking a shift in the middle of the night.

"I'm sure you will do fine. We are all here to help you. This passage will be a team effort. Hopefully, a few days at sea will thrill you."

They both settled into their seats. The sun bathed them in warmth, and the slight breeze provided just enough cooling to make them comfortable.

It seemed they had hardly relaxed when Troy announced it was time for a helm shift change. He called out loudly to Emma to relieve him.

Emma jumped up from the trampoline. Janessa followed, wanting to get a cold beverage from the cooler.

Emma assumed the helm, confident with the transition instructions from Troy and confirming that the navigation had the proper course plotted.

Jordan remained seated on the small corner chair anchored to the railing on the port bow. He was now barefoot and without a shirt. He was gawking at the scenery, especially the awe-inspiring Rock of Gibraltar, still easily within eyesight. His seating position required him to turn his head toward the rear to see the rock correctly. The boat was still within the Straights of Gibraltar, just off the coast of North Africa near Eddalya.

Troy joined Janessa for a cold beverage in the rear salon area. Janessa stood on the raised platform, touching the portside tube. She loosely held the salon roof for balance.

Holding his beverage in his left hand, Troy softly held his right hand on Janessa's backside. They, too, embraced the view of the rock. Janessa looked down into Troy's eyes, smiled, and said, "I love being here with you."

Troy replied, "Yes, I am glad you agreed to join me on this trip."

It had only been about fifteen minutes into Emma's shift when the boat experienced an unusual heaving. It felt like a car going too fast, hitting a speed bump in the middle of the road. All four passengers shifted suddenly.

Emma called out, "What was that?"

Jordan yelled, "Orcas!" the boat heaved a second time. Having already lost her grip from the first jolt, Janessa's complete surprise threw her off balance, over the side, into the calm water. Troy was already on his knees on the salon deck, unable to grab Janessa as she fell overboard. He jumped from kneeling, pulled off his shirt, grabbed the nearby single life preserver, and dived into the water.

Janessa had already surfaced, treading water, and screaming for help. She felt panicked, but understood she needed to calm herself to stay afloat. Her brain told her not to worry about the water, as it was warm with small waves. Still, she was uncertain of what the orcas might do, and the boat's speed was already slowly moving the boat away, creating some distance from her.

Troy swam athletically on his left side with one arm while dragging the single life preserver on the other arm. He rapidly reached Janessa.

159

He placed the life preserve around Janessa, adequately securing it while he wrapped his arms around her, using her flotation as his support.

Janessa was undoubtedly relieved to have Troy embrace her. She felt comforted that he was not only there but enveloping her with his arms. She relaxed, knowing he was there.

They both acknowledged to one another that they were unharmed and able to float acceptably. They expressed concern that the boat was expanding its distance and was still under attack from the orcas.

The second jolt had thrown Jordan onto the trampoline, where he was now attempting to stand. It wasn't easy to stand even when calm, almost like trying to stand on Jello. He could now see another orca approaching a head-on impact with the boat, albeit the whale would swim between the two pontoon hulls. Once between the hulls, the large body mass caused the ship to sway immensely. Jordan fell again, bouncing repeatedly on the trampoline netting.

A rocked Emma kept standing, holding the helm. She scanned the area, counting seven orcas, two of which appeared to be adult females and five juveniles. The two adults seemed to be the aggressors, while the juveniles maintained observation distance.

Jordan interrupted Emma's trance by screaming, "Stop the engines!" Emma immediately turned off the engine's power. Jordan was already scrambling to lower the jib sail. Emma released the line for the mainsail, watching it slide downward.

Meanwhile, Troy and Janessa floated in the water about two hundred yards away. They could see the orcas from their floating perch, but fortunately, none of the beasts paid attention to them. The orcas appeared fully attentive to the boat.

The lack of boat movement now seemed to calm the orcas. Adult orcas made a few slow casual passes near the boat, but nothing that disrupted the ship like the earlier incidents.

Jordan had already hurried to the cockpit with Emma to observe the orcas. Once he realized the orcas were temporarily halting their aggressive actions, he turned his attention to Troy and Janessa. He made hand and arm gestures to communicate with Troy.

He knew Troy was trying to signal him. Still, the distance made it difficult to easily see the hand signs from Troy. Jordan retrieved the Temu 30-260x160 HD binoculars kept in the Navstation cabinet drawer inside the salon, near the galley. These high-power binoculars resembled those he often used onboard navy vessels, and he knew they would undoubtedly be sufficient for his current need.

Jordan quickly spotted Troy and then zoomed in for a close-up view. He could see Troy giving the hand sign for okay, holding his hand with the index and thumb forming a circle. He alternated this hand signal with one showing the international signal for help: holding up four fingers with the thumb tucked across the palm, closing all four fingers over the thumb, and then raising them again. Putting these two hand signals together, Jordan knew that Troy and Janessa were okay but needed help.

Emma shouted, "Look, the orcas are leaving!"

Jordan lowered the binoculars, turning to observe the fleeing orcas. He raised the binoculars to watch the orcas closely as they created meaningful distance from the boat. He assured him they were not making some deceptive movement to return.

Once Jordan felt sure that the orcas had departed and were not returning, he lowered the dinghy into the water. He started the dinghy motor and revved it to maximum power to reach Troy and Janessa as quickly as possible. The little raft promptly skimmed over the top of the calm water.

Before departing, he instructed Emma to assess the boat, especially the rudder, for damage, but had not yet started the engines.

In less than one minute, Jordan reached the two floating victims. He put the engine on idle and pulled Janessa into the dinghy. His first impression was that she was remarkably at ease and, indeed, not distressed, as many inexperienced sailors would be. She composed herself once she sat in the dinghy.

He reached over to assist Troy, who was already showing off his prowess of strength by pulling his body out of the water using the fastened ropes running the length of the inflatable sides of the dinghy.

The three passengers raced the dinghy back to the boat. Emma held a large towel, enveloping Janessa as she stepped onto the deck. She tossed a towel to Troy as he entered. Jordan hooked the dinghy to the pulley system and stepped onto the deck, hoisting it and securing it for the voyage.

Jordan could not help but look at Janessa as she dried herself. His wet shirt clung to her body, revealing her well-shaped breasts. She was not wearing a bra, and her nipples pressed perfectly into her wet shirt.

Emma caught her husband gawking at the thoroughly wet Janessa. She smiled at him and shook her finger affectionately at him.

After spending another thirty minutes getting physically comfortable, thoroughly assessing any boat damage—they found none—and ensuring all safety features and mechanicals were working, they decided to get underway. Emma started the engines. Troy and Jordan helped to raise the mainsail and the jib. Once again, they were motor sailing to the Canary Islands.

Once they were on their way, Emma, standing at the helm, asked the three sitting at the salon deck table, "What caused the orcas to attack the boat?"

Troy quickly responded, "I Googled it while sitting here and what I found is quite interesting."

"Do tell," Janessa said coyly.

"The orcas have been increasing contact with boats for the past few years. They travel in pods that are highly structured matriarchs led by the oldest female. They are often one to three generations. Most boat encounters are near the Iberian Peninsula, most occurring near the Straights of Gibraltar. [84]

They tend to be aggressive towards sailboats that average less than thirty-nine feet and run at slow speeds. Many times, the motor is running," Troy pointed out.

"Okay, but what makes them attack?" asked Jordan

"Well, according to the researchers, they don't like it to be called attacks. They say the orcas are a highly intelligent species and the largest member of the dolphin family. There are two predominant theories. One is that the orcas are playful, curious, and simply racing with the boat.

The other theory is that they may be exercising cautious behavior after some previous traumatic incident. This theory seems to be confirmed because often the adults are the aggressors while the juveniles observe. Perhaps an orca experienced being bumped by a sailboat, and now the adults are teaching the young ones how to avoid and halt the actions of such boats," added Troy.

He paused and continued, "The actions taken to shut off the engines and drop sails are two of the recommended expert actions, along with remaining calm and radioing for help."

"Well, we got three out of four and did not need to radio for help. We had it under control, and the boat undamaged," stated Emma.

The other three raised their glasses, shouted in unison, "Here!"

Emma remained at the helm for another two and a half hours, completing her shift without further incidents. She stepped down from the cockpit, having tuned over the helm to Jordan.

Jordan was at the helm for his three-hour shift, maneuvering the boat past Tangier, Morocco, and around Cap Spartel at the northwest tip of Morocco. Once around the tip, the navigation system plotted its course down the Atlantic coast of Morocco to the Canary Islands. The planned course should be easy to follow. He turned the helm to Janessa, who would now steer the boat for the next three hours, completing the team's first twelve hours and the first round of helmsman shifts.

Troy stood with Janessa for her first thirty minutes, ensuring she understood her responsibilities. His help quickly gave her confidence, and she stood attentively at the helm.

Janessa was about an hour and a half into her shift as the clock approached 7:30 pm. The navigation screen displayed the boat just off the coast of Morocco, near Asilah, a small fishing village. Troy was sitting at the outside salon table, reading a book. Jordan and Emma were inside the small galley preparing dinner.

Janessa watched the radar and scanned the horizon. Then, she suddenly said, "Three boats are heading toward us."

Troy jumped up from the table, bonding quickly to her side in the cockpit. She pointed in the distance off the port bow. Troy grabbed the binoculars, which were still hanging near the helm. He could see three small craft boats speeding from the coast, headed toward their boat. Each of the three boats had four to six passengers. Through the binoculars, Troy could see that the passengers appeared to be local, not tourists, and they were angry.

Troy yelled to Jordan and Emma, "Hey, it looks like we might be in trouble!"

"What is it?" replied Jordan, as he poked his head through the horizontal window.

"I think we have pirates heading in our direction," he stated loudly.

Jordan knew they did not have any weapons on board to defend themselves. He also knew that a sailboat was not about to outrun three small craft speed boats.

Jordan yelled to Janessa, "Janessa, you get down here with Emma!" He turned to Emma and said, "You take Janessa and lock yourselves in our cabin." They hurried inside the cabin, locked the door, and waited anxiously.

Janessa hurried into the salon. She followed Emma quickly into the port side cabin.

Troy called out, "Jordan, get my backpack from my cabin. There's something in it that I think we can use."

Jordan raced to Troy's cabin, quickly finding the backpack. He grabbed it and hurried up to the cockpit, handing the backpack to Troy.

Troy reached inside the bag, pulling out a neat, folded square sheet of cloth. While holding one edge, he flapped it in the slight breeze. The cloth opened to a mid-size United States Naval Academy flag.

Troy shouted, "Hoist this on the mainmast rigging. Perhaps flying it will make the pirates think twice about attacking a boat that flies this flag."

"Good idea!" Jordan shouted.

Jordan barked to Troy to stay at the helm. Jordan turned and bound to the bridge deck. Once there, he attached the flag to the mainmast rigging. It was large enough to be seen at a reasonable distance. He, too, hoped that displaying it might deter potential pirates from attacking a boat affiliated with the United States and, notably, the Naval Academy.

Meanwhile, Troy scrounged a Ka-Bar knife from his backpack. He figured that if the pirates boarded, he would at least have this weapon to defend himself and the others.

Jordan and Troy braced themselves as the three boats surrounded them. One boat was on the port side, the second boat on the starboard side, and the third boat was now at their stern.

The men in all three boats yelled in Arabic and waved their arms. None of them was brandishing any weapons yet, and none of the boats were close enough for any men to make any effort to board their sailing vessel. After only two minutes, a man in the stern boat shouted something in English.

Jordan could not distinguish the exact words, but he was sure they were English. He yelled back, "What is it you want?"

The boat at the stern now approached closer, pulling within twenty yards. Troy remained at the helm, and Jordan jumped down on the stern to communicate more easily with the man in the boat.

He again yelled out, "What is it you want?"

Jordan expected the man to tell him they wanted to board his sailboat. However, he saw that they significantly outnumbered him, and he was still determining what he and

Troy could do if that happened. The man yelled, "Your boat is traveling towards our fishing nets!"

"What?" replied Jordan, unsure that he had fully heard the man, and his tone was not aggressive.

Again, the man yelled, "Your boat is traveling towards our fishing nets. You will tear up our nets, and it will tangle your boat!"

Jordan now understood and was relieved that these were not pirates but local fishermen. He replied, "I understand. What do you want us to do?"

The man said, "Follow us. We'll lead you around our nets."

"Okay," replied Jordan, relieved, but wanting to remain guarded.

Jordan informed Troy of the situation and instructed him to turn the sailboat to follow the speed boats around the waiting fishing nets. He then hustled to the cabin door, telling Emma and Janessa that it was okay to come out.

He explained everything once they were standing in the outside salon deck area. Both girls visibly relaxed, knowing that there was no danger.

These events were the last moments of trouble on their five-day journey to the Canary Islands. The remaining sailing time for the crew passed smoothly. They each took turns at the helm, cooking, cleaning, and relaxing. Janessa advanced well in her helmsmanship duties and increased her sailing knowledge and experience. Most importantly, Emma and Jordan fully briefed Janessa and Troy on the elements of the story, from Henry's video confession to the current sailing adventure.

CHAPTER TWENTY-FOUR
Reaching the Canary Islands

After five days of sailing, the crew glided the boat into Marina Lanzarote, on the northeastern most Canary Islands of Lanzarote, midway on the eastern shore side of the island. They had already reserved a slip.

The marina was a strategic port for sailors traveling south of Europe. Upon arriving in the Canaries, it was the first full-service marina. The city of Arrecife surrounds the marina. Arrecife offers plenty of urban conveniences and local Canary hospitality. The island of Lanzarote displayed a lunar-like landscape. Its dry, volcanic terrain was one of the most barren of the Canaries. It served as an astronaut training location.

They would only have a little time to explore this island. The intention was to spend one full day and night at this marina. This stop would allow time to restock their supplies, get diesel, deal with any minor repairs for the boat, and get some land-based relaxation. Their only exploration would be the close surroundings of Arrecife. [85]

After securing their boat in the reserved slip, they divided duties by drawing assignments from a hat. Troy was first; he drew doing laundry at a local laundromat. On the second draw, Janessa drew the assignment to go to a grocery store for provisions. Emma was third; she drew the assignment of finding the harbormaster to register entry to the Canaries and the country of Spain. Jordan pulled last, getting the assignment for some patching materials for a small tear in the mainsail.

Each crew member set off on their assignments and returned at separate times. Later in the day, they had completed their tasks, cleaned the boat together, and were ready for some relaxation. They showered and groomed to explore the harbor area for fun bars and restaurants.

Fortunately, their boat slip was at the end of the marina dock nearest to the bridge path into town. This boat slip allowed them to avoid the lengthy walk from the far end of the pier. They walked across the Pasarela Bridge, looping onto the Av. Olof Palme. This road traversed a narrow strip of land that separated the marina harbor from the central Arrecife bay. Walking a short distance to the Parque Infantil, they turned onto C. Juan de Quesada. After just two blocks, they found a comfortable location to enjoy a cold beer.

A pure white painted stucco building with blue trim windows and doors sat on the corner. It's royal blue and white striped awning protruded midway up the two-story building, inviting shade to the outside seating area. The outdoor tables were all white acrylic with matching chairs.

They quickly found available seating, and a waiter greeted them, presenting menus. Emma politely informed him they would only order cold beers, not food.

The waiter explained, "I can highly recommend our local craft beer."

"Please enlighten us," replied Janessa.

The waiter explained, "Until recently, we imported all our beers. But within the past few years, we have three local breweries that make local specialty beer. Those breweries are NAO, Bermeja, and Rote. Here at our restaurant, we offer beers brewed by NAO. We have Capitan, an American Pale

Ale; Mucho, an IPA; Hoppyness, a hoppy lager; and Black Patron, a black IPA." [86]

Emma asked, "Do you offer a tasting flight?"

"No, but you could order all four beers, and I will bring you extra glasses, which you can use to create your tasting flight," the waiter proudly offered.

"That is a terrific idea!" exclaimed Janessa.

The waiter left briefly and returned with all four beer choices and sixteen small glasses. He placed four glasses in front of each person and poured approximately three ounces of beer into each glass so that each person had an equal taste of all four beers.

Janessa suggested, "Let's drink the same beer and discuss the various likes and dislikes."

Emma grinned. "That is a wonderful idea."

They arranged their glasses in tasting order for Capitan, Hoppyness, Mucho, and Black IPA. Everyone liked the Capitan. Jordan and Janessa wanted the Hoppyness. Troy and Emma liked the Mucho, and only Emma liked the Black IPA.

After completing the taste test, they called over the waiter to order individual beers. Jordan chose the Capitan, Janessa chose the Hoppyness, and Troy and Emma chose the Mucho.

Basking in the late afternoon sunlight, they enjoyed their refreshing cold beers. They laughed and recanted stories about the passage from Gibraltar.

It seemed odd when they noticed many people and cars on an island that was primarily barren. The busy streets and filled-to-capacity parking lot reminded them that Arrecife was a primary, thriving inhabited area.

They paid their bill and asked the waiter if he had a favorite restaurant different from the one where he worked.

The waiter explained that his favorite restaurant was Barbacana Bar and Grill on the other side of Arrecife Bay, well known for Uruguayan steak. [87] They could take the long route walking around the bay, or they could take the shorter route across the Puenta Charco San Ginés Bridge just down the street from their current location. Once across the bridge, the entire walk would be less than two kilometers.

They thanked the waiter and set out on the shorter route. While crossing the bridge, they could easily see the marina to the east, and if they looked hard enough, they could nearly make out their boat docked in its slip. Turning to the west afforded a view of the entire Arrecife Bay, outlined by buildings surrounding it. The bay formed a nearly perfect circle. Sailboats and other small power craft boats dotted the harbor, moored to floating balls tethered to lines anchored into the harbor bottom.

The walk was moderate, especially since they had just spent five days at sea. They wore various brands of flip-flops, which were comfortable for this short walk. They were all in excellent shape, and this additional exercise felt good. Locating the restaurant took very little time.

The restaurant was perfect. It was in an alleyway, wide enough for vehicles but only available to pedestrians. An oversized garage door-sized opening beckoned patrons to enter the restaurant. A black awning covered the entrance above, and a black sign with gold letters read Barbacana Bar and Grill. Inside, the restaurant decor showed dark wood paneling halfway up the wall and a slight shade of tangerine painted on the upper half of the wall. In the center of the rear wall was a large solid wood bar made of the same wood used for the wall panels. It also had a copper metal top.

There are about twelve tables with four or six chairs neatly arranged around the bar. The restaurant offered four outside tables with four chairs, each sitting in the brick-paved pedestrian alleyway. There were other restaurants in the alley that offered similar seating.

They chose the only remaining outside table. The table, made of dark black wood, held four light mahogany-stained wooden chairs that stood at each side. Each chair had a solid bottom and slated mid-back support.

Their arrival was just at the crest of nightfall. A slight late summer breeze blew through the alley, making it very comfortable. The lights from the alley restaurants created a golden glow in the alley.

When the waiter arrived, they quickly ordered a beer, already knowing the NAO beer choices on the menu. They each chose the same single beer they had at the previous place. They each also ordered the same steak dinner. Three of them requested their steak medium rare, and only Janessa ordered her steak well done.

The steaks arrived just as they were finishing their first beers. The food presentation was simple: a grilled steak in the center of an oblong, white acrylic plate with a pile of thick-cut potato fries on the left and a spread of fried pickles to the right.

After consulting with the waiter about wine, they learned that El Grifo, the oldest winery in the Canary Islands and the eighth oldest in Spain, still operated on the island of Lanzarote. [88]

The winery grew grapes locally on vines planted in crater-like pits called hoyos. The hoyos protected the grapes from harsh winds while allowing them to maintain moisture and access to sunlight. They mainly grew Listán Negro and Volcanic Malvasia grapes, from which they made both white and red wines.

Their waiter suggested they order a bottle of the Listán Negro Grano a Grano. It was a medium red wine that tasted of cherries and smelled of white flowers. It was silky across the tongue and light on tannins.

They quickly finished one bottle of the suggested wine and ordered a second to accompany their meals. They commented on the outstanding taste of the steaks.

After finishing their meals, they returned to the marina, enjoying the cool night air. They effortlessly found the boat. They said good night and settled into their cabins for a restful sleep.

The next morning, they would make the nearly fourteen-hour sail to the lower end of the island of Fuerteventura. Once there, they could visit Casa Winter.

CHAPTER TWENTY-FIVE
Exploring Casa Winter

They motored into Puerto de Morro Jable, on the southeast side of Fuerteventura Island. They had good winds for sailing, making the trip in about thirteen hours. It was nearly 10:00 pm.

To enter the port, one needed to hook around the man-made jetty, which created the barrier for the docking slips. The jetty allowed for the docking of one mid-size cruise ship, one of which was already docked. Multi-story deck lights provided additional lighting across the harbor entrance.

Docking slips were in the back corner of the marina. They temporarily moored the boat to a dock cleat. Jordan went to locate the dockmaster to obtain their reserved slip assignment.

After nearly twenty minutes, Jordan returned. He pointed across the short distance to the first of three docking piers. Most of the slips accommodated only monohull sailboats or mid-size motorboats. Each dock had four slips at the end, wide enough to allow a catamaran to dock. Their assigned slip was at the end of the first dock.

Troy maneuvered the catamaran into its assigned slip. Emma and Jordan secured the rope lines to the cleats. Janessa positioned the bumpers to prevent the boat hull from banging into the dock.

It was nearly 11:00 pm when they fully secured the boat. They agreed they were all too tired to adventure into town. In fact, they were too tired to prepare a proper dinner. Instead, they slumped into the boat's seats and opened four beers, a bag of chips, a wedge of blue cheese, and wheat-thin crackers. They enjoyed their evening snacks and headed off to bed for much needed sleep. The plan was to drive the following day to Casa Winter.

After waking early, they showered, dressed, and groomed for a casual day of exploration. They ate a quick breakfast that included bagels, cream cheese, granola, apples, and grapes.

They departed together, walking a short distance to the Enterprise rental car building next to the public bathroom building just outside the dock area. Jordan went inside to execute the paperwork while the other three waited outside.

Jordan returned with keys to a white Jeep Renegade. It was a four-door subcompact SUV with 4x4 off-road capability. The vehicle was comfortable for the four explorers and their day packs.

Before departing, Jordan had unfolded a map and placed it on the Jeep hood. He pointed out that they must travel to Carretera Punta de Jandia. This unpaved road headed further south towards the Fuerteventura lighthouse at the island's south end.

About halfway there, they would find another unpaved road with no name, heading west across the island and over the mountain ridge towards Mirador Cofete, which would have fantastic panoramic views out towards the ocean.

They would follow the road to the small town of Cofete and then to Casa Winter. The entire drive should take less than one hour.

It was a beautiful, sunny morning. The sky was a gentle blue with puffy, white clouds, and the wind was moderate.

They encountered an absolutely barren, volcanic terrain upon leaving the Morro Jabal area. The road was indeed unpaved. The road was a windswept-packed volcanic rock cut into the terrain by the weight of vehicles that traveled over it. They drove with the windows up and the air-conditioning turned on because of the wind kicking up dust.

After roughly thirty minutes, they found the turnoff to the road across the island and a sign that read Cofete. After another twenty minutes, they arrived in the desolate town of Cofete. [89]

Cofete was so small that they were unsure it could be called a town. They commented on the few single-story buildings, many of which looked more like sheds, and the large wire fence that surrounded everything. The trim paint on any building faded completely from the wind and the sun.

They did see a restaurant that looked acceptable. They may stop there after visiting Casa Winter.

In the blink of an eye, they were on the other side of the town. They could now see Casa Winter. They could also see the breach and ocean to their west. The terrain sloped upward from the beach to the villa and beyond, where it then jutted upward to the mountain peak. Casa Winter stood about halfway up the slope.

The villa stood regally in an otherwise desolate patch of landscape. Not a single growth of vegetation was present. It was apparent now why the Germans had selected this desolate tract to build the villa.

They still had about a fifteen-minute drive to reach the villa. From a distance, it was easy to see the white stucco building with its turret on the northwest corner. A long volcanic stone wall protected the front of the structure. The mountain stood majestically behind the villa.

They reached the villa, parked the Jeep, and absorbed the panorama. As desolate as the landscape was, the view of the beach and ocean below was beautiful. The breeze brought a unique smell, a combination of ocean and volcanic soil.

Jordan pointed to the beach below, addressing the group. "Look there at the beach. It's too shallow for any submarine to surface or to dock there."

Emma replied, "I agree. There was a rumor that this villa had secret submarine docking capability. But now, seeing the surroundings firsthand, capability could not have maintained here."

The group proceeded to the main entrance. The director of the property, who informed them that there would be a fee for touring the property, greeted them. She gave them a guide map, a history document, and a brief verbal review of the property and its history. She pointed out the direction to proceed and informed them she would be available to answer questions at the end of their self-guided tour.

They made their way through the kitchen, the grand room, the living quarters, and the turret. They climbed the stairs to the top, where they exited to a rooftop view. The panoramic view was grander than the one from the parking lot.

After fully traversing the primary and second floors, the tour route took them to the basement or lower floors. The floor structure grabbed their attention. This floor contained separate rooms, appearing much like a hospital. The walls were now stained and dirty. But it was easy to determine that the walls made of white porcelain tile once stood exceptionally clean and sterile.

The guide map described that the large room contained rows of hospital beds, a couple of small room offices, and yet another room, the surgery room. It further stated that private surgeries of various types took place here near the end of WWII. The staff performed plastic surgery as one of the most common types of surgery. That fact certainly caught Emma's attention.

Emm turned to her friends, stating, "Based upon what we have already uncovered, it is very likely that Adolf Hitler and Eva Braun came here to Casa Villa. Do you think they had plastic surgery performed here in this room?"

"I think it is highly likely," replied Jordan.

They finished their view of the surgery room and proceeded into the next room, which the map described as the head surgeon's office. It was a simple twelve-by-twelve-foot room with three white-painted plaster walls and one lava stone wall.

A carving rested in the center of the lava stone wall. The guide map made no special mention of this carving. Janessa briefly examined the carving, and Troy also took a quick look. It mesmerized Jordan and stared at it for over ten minutes.

"What so intrigues you about that carving?" asked Emma.

With a puzzled look, Jordan said, "There is something about this carving that makes me think there is more to it than a simple carving." He pauses and turns to the others. "All of you, come over here."

The three friends gathered around Jordan, who began describing the carving. "Look at the moons carved across the top. These are the eight phases of the moon: new moon, waxing crescent, first quarter, waxing gibbous, full moon, waning gibbous, third quarter, and waning crescent. [90]

Under the eight moons are two horses, one facing left and the other facing right. Each horse has a rider. The rider is a human body, wrapped in a fur coat, with a beast head showing horns sticking through a helmet."

"Okay, so what?" asked Troy.

Jordan quickly responds, "We have found several times that the Germans put things into codes and used codes to lock guarded vaults."

Emma jumped in. "You think this is another secret code?"

"Yes, I do," replied Jordan.

Janessa asked, "What do you think it is telling us?"

"I think the beast represents Hitler. The letter H is the eighth letter in the alphabet, represented by the eight phases of the moon. There are two beasts and two horses, which suggests two times eight for sixteen or eight twice. I think it's eight twice for the number eighty-eight, which is known as HH or Heil Hitler by neo-Nazi groups." Jordan stated confidently. [91]

"Okay, I buy that," said Troy. "But what do we do with that?"

"I don't know yet." Jordan frowned.

Janessa moved her hand lightly across the carving, using her fingers to outline the figures gently. After twice covering the entire carving, she turned to Jordan and said, "There is something about the horse's eye. One eye seemed to wiggle a little."

Janessa took Jordan's' right hand and placed his index finger on the right-facing horse's eye. She pressed his finger to the stone eye. Indeed, he felt it nudge.

Jordan exclaimed, "We need something to clear the dirt around the two horse eyes."

They each fumbled around in their pockets but found nothing. Janessa had carried her backpack, primarily for the water bottle within it. She dug into the pack, pulling out a metal nail file and a small makeup brush. She proudly stretched her hand to Jordan, said, "Will these do?"

Jordan looked excited. "I think those will work." He used the tools to dig, scratch, and brush away the dirt surrounding each horse-eye. When he finished, he handed the tools back to Janessa.

"Now, what is next?" Troy asked.

"I think we are to push each horse eye eight times," responded Jordan. He then turned to the carving and pushed each eye eight times, but nothing happened. He turned to his friends and looked puzzled.

Emma said, "Maybe we should press each eye eight times simultaneously."

Jordan reached out to hug her. "You are wonderful." He then brought her forward to the carving and placed her index finger on the left-facing horse eye and his index finger on the right-facing horse eye. Jordan slowly counted to eight, with the two each pressing the horse's eyes simultaneously after each stated sequential number. Upon reaching the number eight, the stone carving jarred slightly, revealing a perfect square outline cut into the wall. The stone carving jarred outward just enough to allow Jordan to grab the edges with his fingers and pull outward.

His effort revealed a drawer hidden inside the rock wall. The four peered into the drawer and beamed with excitement. Inside the drawer was a stack of files and boxes containing gold teeth, jewelry, such as rings, necklaces, and watches.

Before they alerted the villa director or before other touring people might enter the room, they wanted to review the files themselves quickly. Jordan instructed all of them to use their phones to take pictures of all the items in the drawer and all the papers in the files. They could look at those later.

After hurriedly completing their assignments, Emma went to retrieve the villa director. Emma explained what they had found and how they discovered the drawer. The director hurried back with Emma.

This unique finding astounded the director. She would need to report it to the island's Spanish authorities. Meanwhile, she would close this room off from any further tourist visits. The director thanked the foursome and escorted them outside.

They hurried across the parking lot to the Jeep. Each one guarded the phones as if they were sacred objects. They drove quickly down the road back to the small town of Cofete, to the restaurant they had seen earlier.

They pulled into the parking lot of Restaurant Cofete Pepe El Faro. [92] There were only three other compact cars parked in the lot. It was simply a cleared area in the volcanic rock, unpaved, like the road.

The restaurant building looked well-kept but worn. Faded orange or red paint exhibited a long-ago facelift, much like the surrounding buildings.

Upon entering, they quickly noticed how clean and quaint it looked inside. They walked across the floor, tiled with gray and brown stones. The owner used the same stones in another pattern to tile a third of each wall with fresh white paint on the remaining wall area.

Many local artifacts and pictures hung along all the painted walls.

Small and rectangular tables, made of wooden stained light oak, accompanied by four matching chairs, provided adequate seating for their needs. There were ten of these tables and a bar spanning across the small room.

In the back, one could easily spot the kitchen. There was a strong smell of garlic and fried food permeating the air.

Umbrellas shade the outside tables and chairs, but the team chose one of the inside corner tables. This secluded table would afford them additional privacy as two walls guarded it.

They sat down and anxiously pulled out their phones. However, the waitress appeared quickly, which caused them to delay reviewing their pictures. The waitress asked, "Can I bring you something cold to drink?"

"A cold beer would be nice. What do you recommend?" Troy asked.

The waitress replied, "I suggest the Estrella Damm. It is a nice lager, brewed in Barcelona." She then pointed to a sign above the bar. "See the sign with the star. Estrella means star and the name Damm is the name of the original brewmaster August Küntzmann Damm." [93]

"We will take four," Troy said.

They continued to wait to review their phone pictures, as they knew the waitress would be returning shortly with the beer order. Meanwhile, they looked over the menu.

Emma was quick to point out a unique feature of the menu. "Look at the menu. The menu showed items presented in three languages: Spanish, English, and German. It appears there remains a strong German influence on this island."

The waitress arrived with their beers and four glasses. Troy was quick to pour and taste his. "This is an excellent beer. It has a fresh taste, some lively acidity, and it finishes with a slightly bitter and long-lasting taste."

The others quickly poured theirs, tasted, and nodded in agreement. They placed their food orders.

They now felt refreshed and ready to get on with the review of their pictures. Each person set their phone in the center of the table. They positioned the phones so that all four could see the photos from the proper angle.

They reviewed Emma's phone first. She swiped through her pictures. They revealed the initial content of the drawer, which showed the jewelry and the files.

She had photos of four files, which she presented to the team. The files contained names of patients, each one showing a German officer, original facial pictures, post-operative facial pictures, surgeon notes, copies of new identity papers, and others.

They did not recognize the names of these four German officers. Still, the exactness of the record keeping intrigued them.

Jordan next reviewed his photos. He had five files to present. Like the ones Emma presented, they contained the same type of information about four German officers and one woman, the wife of one officer.

Again, though, nothing about these five individuals really meant anything to them.

Janessa was the third to present her photos. She had four total files to present. Janessa had already reviewed two files with the same results as Emma and Jordan.

She swiped to the picture for the third file, and immediately, all four gasped with eyes wide open. The file jacket picture displayed the name of Adolf Hitler. They pushed their faces closer to look.

Janessa swiped through the photos, each revealing information like the previously reviewed files. These pictures showed that Adolf Hitler had facial plastic surgery at Casa Winter in May 1945 and that following his surgery, he journeyed to Tenerife in early June to connect with a U-boat to travel to Argentina. They also learned that he changed his name to Adolf Schuttlemayer.

The last file presented by Janessa was equally intriguing. The name on that file jacket was Eva Braun. They learned that she, too, had facial plastic surgery, and that she changed her name to Eve Schuttlemayer, the wife of Adolf Schuttlemayer. She accompanied him on the journey to Argentina. [94]

They might discover additional salacious information, so they looked closely at Troy's five files. These files represented three German officers, two wives, and contained information similar to those in the previous files.

They commented on much of the similarity in the information in each file. All eighteen people had surgery, changed their names, and had new identities. The one additional thing that they identified as a common thread was that all of them were being transported to Argentina to start new lives.

The waitress interrupted them, bringing their food. It included a shared plate of parmesan-covered grilled scallops, two cheeseburgers for Jordan and Troy, garlic shrimp for Emma, and bronzed fish of the day for Janessa. They ordered another round of Estrella Damm beer.

After finishing their surprisingly delicious meal, they loaded back into the Jeep for the ride back to the marina in Morro Jabal. It only took them about forty minutes to reach the marina, where they returned to the rental car and strolled over to their boat. They enjoyed a relaxing evening on the boat with a couple of bottles of wine and munchies again. They would depart again the following day.

Previously, they had planned to go to the island of Tenerife. But they determined the team would gain nothing additional by going there. Instead, they would leave the boat docked at the Morro Jabal marina. Jordan had already contacted the rental company and arranged for the sailboat to be left there.

They would travel one hour north on a paved road to the Fuerteventura Airport by taxi. They would need to travel lengthy distances to reach their destinations.

Jordan and Emma would have a nearly forty-five-hour flight from Fuerteventura to Frankfort, then Frankfurt to Buenos Aires, and finally Buenos Aires to San Carlos de Bariloche, Argentina.

Troy and Janessa would have almost thirty-six hours from Fuerteventura to Zurich, Zurich to Chicago, and finally, Chicago to Norfolk, Virginia. Once in Norfolk, they would have about one hour by car back to Hampton.

Fortunately, both parties' flights depart early to midafternoon. Therefore, they could travel together to the island airport.

CHAPTER TWENTY-SIX

Onward to Bariloche, Argentina

They arrived at the Fuerteventura Airport almost three hours before Jordan and Emma's flight. Troy and Janessa would have an additional hour to wait. They all wanted to give themselves ample time.

Pleasantly surprised by the modernness of the clean, lovely airport, they quickly got their baggage checked in and through security. For an island, the airport was large but easily manageable. It was two floors with twenty-four boarding gates, fifteen baggage carousels, eleven retail stores, and twelve eating and drinking establishments.

Having already eaten, they wanted a smaller meal. They had already eaten a hearty breakfast on board the boat and planned for a sustenance meal when they reached their first layover stop. After briefly walking the passenger concourse, they found the Market Square Coffee Shop. It served coffee, tea, and primarily, pastries and cakes. It was the perfect place to get a light snack and kill time. [95]

While waiting for two hours, they consumed a coffee latte and various parties. They joked, laughed, and regaled stories about the adventure from Gibraltar to the Canary Islands. Supplementing the festive stories, they also summarized their findings at Casa Winter and discussed Jordan and Emma's plan for reaching Bariloche, Argentina.

Fifty-One. It was in the next building adjacent to the hotel. It offered sushi, Argentinian, and South American dishes.

Jordan and Emma dined early, knowing they needed to get up well before sunrise for their flight. They dined on two sushi rolls and a plate of Argentina BBQ ribs with fries.

The hotel shuttle transported them to the airport at 2:30 am the following morning. Scheduled to depart at 4:50 am, they would arrive in San Carlos de Bariloche at 7:55 am. This arrival time would afford them an entire day to get acquainted with Bariloche. Jordan had already reserved two nights of lodging at Charming Luxury Lodge and Personal Spa.

The two-and-one-half-hour flight was certainly short compared to the other ones already taken for this part of the journey. They arrived on time at the Teniente Luis Candelaria International Airport. They retrieved their baggage and secured the Budget rental car. It was a PE 4x4 Renault Duster SUV, bronze colored with a beige leather interior. Well-equipped with cruise control, climate zone control, heated seats, and a simple navigation system, the car's assets would be helpful.

They loaded the Duster and navigated to their hotel, Charming Luxury Lodge and Private Spa, about thirty minutes away. It was at the cliff of Playa Bonita, just fifteen minutes west of the downtown area. [99] As they drove through the downtown streets, Emma commented, "So much of the architecture has a Swiss alpine feeling."

"Of course it does. There were quite a few Germans who migrated here both before the war and afterward," he replied.

They arrived at the lodge. The owners built it on a bluff of a cliff, with panoramic vistas of Lake Nahuel and the Andes Mountain range. Wood and stone comprised the structure, giving it an authentic, small, alpine village look. Each suite had its own balcony suspended over the bluff, which made it easy to see the waves crashing below upon Playa Bonita beach.

They checked in, dropped their luggage in their suite, and headed back to the Duster to drive into town. They wanted to acclimate and explore.

Jordan found a parking facility beside the Shopping Patagonia shopping mall in the center of town. Eager shoppers crowded the mall and many of the streets. They stopped at a local chocolate store for a local treat. People knew Bariloche for its chocolate, which reflected another solid German influence. The shopkeeper informed them it would be more crowded later in the day when the skiers returned from Cerro Catedral Ski Resort, which was about one hour away. [100] Many skiers preferred to stay in town as more restaurants and bars were available.

The shopkeeper also informed them that there was a local history museum a few blocks away that might be of interest. He also advised that they visit the cathedral and the park at the lakeshore.

Before they left the shopping mall, they found a store selling gloves, something they had forgotten the day before. They quickly each found a pair of suitable gloves, a kind of five-finger ski gloves, not mittens.

Emma suggested they first walk the seven blocks to the cathedral and park. The air was clear, with just enough coldness to see one's breath. However, the walk invigorated her body, and she felt comfortable in her new winter clothes. She grabbed Jordan's gloved hand, and they walked hand in hand to the cathedral.

"No, the actual artist did not sign it. The name inscribed is Raphael," the clerk said.

Before Jordan or Emma asked another question, the clerk told them, "You can visit the gravestone of Adolf Schuttlemayer and Eve at the park near the cathedral in town."

Emma and Jordan thanked the woman and hurried back to their parked Duster. Jordan started the engine and was about to pull away when three black Mercedes G-class SUVs surrounded their vehicle.

CHAPTER TWENTY-SEVEN
Hostage

Six men exited the three SUVs. The drivers remained in each vehicle. Men dressed in black trousers, gray tee shirts, and black leather jackets rushed toward Emma and Jordan and brandished pistols aimed at the two sleuths.

One man shouted at them to exit the vehicle. Jordan and Emma cautiously opened the doors and stood outside the car. Two men approached each victim, placing a black hood over their heads.

The men tied Jordan and Emma's hands behind their backs and pulled them to the Mercedes, pushing them inside.

They placed Emma in one Mercedes, in the rear seat, between two thugs. Jordan rode in a second Mercedes, seated similarly. The third Mercedes drove at the rear of the line.

Driving for nearly one hour on paved roads, they turned onto a gravel path. They followed that route for almost another thirty minutes. It felt as though they were climbing upward on this route.

The vehicles stopped. Assailants dragged Jordan and Emma from the cars and pushed forward. Jordan stopped abruptly and shouted, "Emma, are you there?"

Emma answered, "Yes. Are you okay?"

Before Jordan could answer, one man punched him in the stomach, causing him to bend over, gasping for breath.

Another man shouted at them to be quiet.

Gravel crunched under their feet as they walked. Their bodies shivered from the cooler air of the higher altitude. They climbed four steps and waited. They could hear one man speaking into an intercom and the voice instructing them to bring the guests to the assembly room.

Jordan thought to himself that he hardly felt like a guest.

Emma knew Jordan was near, as she could hear his breathing and footsteps. His presence gave her some reassurance.

She sensed being in a hallway. She heard the noise of their footsteps bounce more quickly as they walked a short distance and then waited. Emma could hear metal doors gliding on a track. Someone pushed her forward. She stumbled a bit, thinking she might be falling. Emma regained balance, listened to the doors close, and sensed movement. She realized she was descending in an elevator.

Again, the doors opened, and someone pushed her to move forward. Emma felt the flooring variations beneath her feet, moving from hard surface to carpet and back to hard surface. She could hear voices getting louder as she walked. Emma smelled wood burning and could hear the crackle of burning logs.

Emma felt a hand push on her chest as a voice shouted to sit down. Once seated, a thug secured her wrists to the chairs' arms and tied her ankles. He removed the hood covering her head. Her eyesight somewhat blurred, taking a few seconds to focus clearly. Before concentrating on her surroundings, she turned her head to locate Jordan. He was now sitting to her right, bound to a chair like herself.

Their eyes met. Emm immediately asked, "Are you alright?"

Jordan replied, "Yes. I am fine, and you?"

Emma said, "Yes, I am okay."

A voice from farther away boomed, demanding they all remain quiet! They both turned their attention toward the voice and stared.

A slender man in his mid-forties approached from across the room. He wore denim jeans, soft-soled black leather shoes, and a gray turtleneck covered by a black wool sweater.

He said, "Welcome. I am Martin Schuttlemayer. I have been looking forward to meeting you."

Emma abruptly asked, "What do you want? Why are we being tied up?"

Martin replied, "I have some questions for you."

Martin turned, looking across the room. He asked someone seated there if he should continue. The voice instructed him to move onward indeed.

Meanwhile, Jordan assessed their surroundings. They were in a rather large room. There were no windows, and the knowledge that they descended in the elevator meant they were probably in some below-earth room.

A fireplace and comfortable seating area appeared at one end of the room, similar to someone's living room. There were five men seated there. That's where the most recent voice emanated.

The walls were all dark stained wood panels. Paintings hung neatly arranged along the walls. Statues, sculptures, and other silver and gold figures adorned shelves and tables throughout the room.

They sat in two chairs at the opposite end of the room, separated by tables. It hardly seemed like a place to hold prisoners.

Martin proceeded, "You were the two who caused the arrest of Peter Müller."

He paused. "Peter was one of our greatest benefactors."

The voice boomed, "Son, get on with it!"

Emma smugly asked, "So, who is that?"

Martin replied, "Not that you need to know. But it is my father, Dieter Schuttlemayer."

Emma could now smell the scent of a cigar wafting in the air.

Martin asked, "Why are you here in Bariloche?"

Neither Emma nor Jordan immediately answered. Standing close to Jordan, Martin used a black leather glove to slap Jordan across the face. Jordan flinched and quickly shot a glare at Martin.

Emma snapped, "We are here on a ski trip!"

Martin snorted, "Do not lie to me. I know your trip is not a simple ski holiday." He again asked, "Why are you here?"

And once again, Emma, attempting to be coy, stated, "I told you we are here for a ski trip and nothing else."

Dieter moved towards them, walking indignantly. Without saying a word, he stood next to Jordan, puffing his cigar. When the cigar was glowing hot, he placed the red ember on the back of Jordan's left hand, burning the flesh.

Jordan screamed, "Motherfucker!" The pain was immediate and intense. The smell was horrid.

Dieter shouted, "No more stalling! You will answer our questions, or we will subject you to more pain." He turned and motioned to another man to come over to them.

The man approached and Dieter said, "Herr Doctor, please prepare your tools should they need them."

The doctor placed a leather bundle on the table and rolled it open. Now lying in plain sight was a series of knives, pliers, ice picks, and other cutting instruments. He set a butane torch upright on the table.

Dieter nodded to the doctor. The doctor lit the torch, and the blue flame shot from the funnel, sounding like a small jet engine. He walked to Jordan's chair, facing him.

Without further hesitation, the doctor quickly placed the burning flame into the wound already visible in Jordan's left hand. Jordan screamed, "You son of a bitch!"

The doctor continued to burn a hole through Jordan's hand. The flame reached the wood of the chair arm on which Jordan's hand rested. Jordan fainted.

Simultaneously, Emma screamed, "stop!"

She paused, sobbed slightly, and said, "Just stop. I will tell you whatever you want to know."

Jordan began to wake from his momentary unconscious sleep. He looked at Emm as she answered questions.

Martin opened, "What are you doing here?"

Emma answered, "We came here to discover if Adolf Hitler escaped to this town following WWII."

"And why would you think that?" asked Martin.

"Because we found information at Villa Winter, in the Canary Islands that showed Adolf Hitler and Eva Braun received facial surgery at the Villa and then journeyed to Argentina, settling here in Bariloche," replied Emma.

"So, there is no other reason you are here?" asked Martin.

Emma shook her head, "No."

Martin nodded to the doctor, who again lowered the flame towards Jordan. "She is telling the truth!" Screamed Jordan.

Emma screeched, "What do you think we are doing here?"

Martin scorned, "That is not for you to know."

Dieter interjected. "We know you found one of our treasure troves in Basel. Your discovery caused the arrest of Peter Müller. We followed you to Villa Winter and then here to Argentina. You are here to track us and to thwart our current plan for causing terrorism in the United States."

Martin turned abruptly. "Why are you telling them this?"

Dieter returned. "It matters not. We will kill them anyway."

Emma glared. "You know Jordan is an active-duty officer in the United States Navy. Any harm to him will certainly bring future investigation by the Navy."

Dieter turned his attention back to Emma. He stated, "We already have agents inserted throughout the United States. They have been crossing over your southern border for over a year.

We have resurrected Operation Pastorius. Like its original intention, we intend to blow up and destroy several targets throughout the United States. We intend to make it appear that Middle East terrorists complete the tragedies.

These events will cause further unrest throughout your country, hopefully with more blame towards the Middle East. We intend to use this world's uncertainty to begin our efforts to take over the country of Germany and once again bring the Nazi party to power."

Martin added, "We don't need the two of you meddling in our plans."

Dieter ordered, "Leave them. Let's meet at the other end of the room to discuss matters."

Jordan looked at Emm, still wincing in pain, "Don't worry. Hopefully, we can hold out a bit longer."

CHAPTER TWENTY-EIGHT

Hello Again, Inspector Gaudot

Outside the mountain chalet, men exited from several vehicles. The men dressed in camouflage fatigues, helmets, and protective vests. They armed themselves with military weapons. They primarily carried pistols. Some men wore jackets with visible letters for identification.

Inspector Gaudot conversed with the leader of the local Argentine police and a United States Navy SEAL officer. They coordinated their efforts to breach the chalet.

Gaudot, holding out his iPhone, said, "See, this is the location of the GPS tracker signal."

Gaudot explained that when Jordan and Emma left Basel, he and Jordan placed a GPS tracker device in the shoe for both Emma and Jordan. When Jordan reached Argentina, he called Gaudot, asking, as a precaution, that Gaudot fly to Argentina and keep a close watch on them.

This tracker device had an alarm feature. Jordan triggered the alarm when the thugs first apprehended him and Emma. The alarm trigger alerted Gaudot to trouble. Gaudot contacted the local Argentine police in Bariloche for assistance. He also reached the United States Embassy in Buenos Aires.

They communicated to the Secretary of the Navy because Jordan was an active-duty officer in trouble. The Navy sent orders to Guantanamo Bay, Cuba, where a SEAL team deployed for training and waited for assignment. [104] A typical commercial flight would be almost nine hours. However, the SEAL team, flying on an urgent United States Air Force mission, made the trip in about seven hours.

Assembled outside the chalet, the SEAL team would be the primary group to breach the chalet, followed by the police. The plan assigned the police to surround the chalet. Gaudot and other plain-clothed officials would be the last to enter.

Everyone was in position. Gaudot gave the order, "Go! Go!"

The SEAL team, using C4 explosives, blew open the large front door. They immediately entered.

Without firing a shot, they quickly secured several people moving about the house. They would later learn these people were all simply servants: the butler, the chef, the maid, and the gardener. None of them had anything to do with Emma and Jordan's apprehension or the business of the chalet owner.

Meanwhile, in the underground basement room, one thug, looking at a video screen, shouted, "We have trouble. The military is here!"

The other men raced to the monitor. It was clear the military planned to breach the chalet. They could also determine, by moving through camera positions, that spies surrounded the house.

Dieter ordered, "Quickly, gather everything. We must leave."

Martin asked, "What about them?" He pointed to Emma and Jordan.

Dieter replied, "Have one of the men finish them." Dieter pressed a button on the table to open a door in the wall. They hurried to it and descended a long flight of stairs.

The stairs led to a small tram they used on a narrow-gauge railway through the mountain. The destination was on the other side of the mountain, several miles from the chalet and completely undetected.

There, the Nazi group loaded into black Mercedes G-class SUVs hidden in a secret garage. They raced away.

Back in the chalet basement room, the thug left behind grabbed a knife from the doctor's tool kit and moved to shove it into Emma's chest. Before he could reach her, Emma, using her leg strength, stood and turned the chair backward, using the chair legs to attack the thug.

Jordan joined the fight, using the same technique. Together, they thwarted the man, pinning him against the wall.

Upstairs, Gaudot entered the house. He questioned the servants about Emma and Jordan. They still need to provide solid answers. The maid volunteered to say an elevator led to a sub-level room. She showed the location of the button to Gaudot.

He pushed the button. The wall moved, revealing metal doors, which then opened. He, the seal team officer, the police captain, and three additional men entered the elevator and descended.

The doors opened. The group of men swiftly exited. They raced across the room to assist Emma and Jordan, who were now holding one thug against the wall.

The SEAL team leader cut the cords binding Emma's and Jordan's hands and feet. He radios to one of his men upstairs to bring the medical kit, as Jordan needed medical attention.

Jordan told Gaudot, "We sure are glad to see you again."

Gaudot smiled, "Good that I got here in time."

Emma hugged Gaudot. She then hugged Jordan and placed a proper kiss on his lips.

The SEAL team medic attended to Jordan's wound. He explained to Jordan that he would get additional medical attention when they transported him to a hospital. He will require some surgery, skin grafts, and physical therapy.

Emma explained to her rescuers what had transpired since their capture. Most importantly, she informed them about the Schuttlemayers and their plan to carry-out terrorist acts in the United States.

They moved over to the meeting area of the room, looking for anything that the Nazi group left behind. Gaudot found one page of paper under the sofa. The paper had a picture of a man, a brief biography, and a short summation of his deployment mission to the United States.

Emma found a writing pad on the table. It was blank. She spied a pencil, which she used to shade over the first page of the tablet. It displayed a list of strategically located United States cities. Boston, New York City, Atlanta, Dallas, Phoenix, San Francisco, Seattle, and Chicago were those cities.

The SEAL team leader called on a satellite phone. He spoke directly with the Secretary of the Navy, explaining that they had rescued Emma and Jordan and that they had uncovered a plan for terrorist actions in the United States. He hung up and instructed Emma and Jordan that he was under orders to bring the two of them to CIA headquarters in Langley immediately.

Emma turned her head, focusing on a specific painting hanging on the wall. It was the *Portrait of a Young Man by Raphael*. This one was undoubtedly the original. She beamed and called Jordan to see the painting. Turning to Gaudot, Emma pointed out the painting and suggested that the other artworks, sculptures, and artifacts in the room were likely all stolen Nazi treasure. Gaudot assured her he would personally see to the inventory and security of everything.

Emma and Jordan again thanked Gaudot and said goodbye. The SEAL team whisked them away.

En route to the airport, Emma requested the seal team officer. "Would it be possible to take a slight detour to the church in Bariloche? It will only take a few minutes, and it's on the way to the airport."

Jordan asked her, "Why do you want to do that?"

She replied, "I want to see the headstone of Adolf Schuttlemayer."

The team leader agreed as long as it was going to be quick.

They quickly drove sixty minutes back to town, finding a parking spot near the park.

Emma and Jordan walked to the cathedral's front steps and entered inside to find the small retail store clerk inside. They inquired of her about the headstone.

The clerk politely responded that there was a single headstone at the northeast end of the park. There are no other headstones because the park isn't a cemetery. The town council approved a unique appeal from Adolf Schuttlemayer and his wife, allowing only them to be buried there because they were great benefactors.

Emma ran outside around the corner of the cathedral and peered towards the northeast corner. She pointed to the far northeast corner of the park. "It looks like some sort of granite block out there."

With his good right hand, Jordan grabbed her hand and started walking quickly to that section of the park. Indeed, they found a large, square granite headstone facing out to the lake. It was a beautiful location.

They looked at the headstone, reading the names of Adolf Schuttlemayer and Eve Schuttlemayer.

Still holding Emma's hand, Jordan suggested she look closely at the headstone. "Look at the top edge of the headstone."

Emma leaned in closer to get a good view. She turned to Jordan and gasped.

Jordan realized she had also now discovered it too, and said, "There is a carved eighty-eight on the top edge of the headstone. That can only mean one thing."

"For sure," Emma said to Jordan, and smiled. They hurried back to the waiting vehicle.

For the next twenty-minute drive to the airport, they said little. After boarding the waiting Air Force plane, it promptly took off for Guantanamo, where the plane refueled, and then onward to Langley.

CHAPTER TWENTY-NINE
A Visit to Langley

Emma and Jordan walked through the main door of the CIA headquarters building, accompanied by the SEAL team leader, Captain Freeman. The Langley team needed the captain for the full debriefing.

A polite young female CIA agent greeted them. She handed them each a visitor badge and escorted them to the elevator. They ascended three floors, where they exited, and another agent took them to a large conference room.

Upon entering, the agent introduced them to the team waiting there. It included the Secretary of the Navy, Admiral Carlson; the CIA Director, George Dickens; the head of the FBI, Stan Perkins; two FBI agents, Beth Sommers, and Kevin Kahn; two CIA agents, Kelsey Hill, and Scott Gamble, and a CIA technician, Casandra Jones. The Secretary of Homeland Security, Robert Deeks, along with the other members of the Joint Chiefs of Staff and members of the National Security Council, was at the White House with the President.

Admiral Carlson was a big man. He stood nearly six feet four inches, the tallest man in the room. The Admiral had broad shoulders and appeared in fine physical condition, given he was nearly seventy-one. He enlisted in the Navy right out of high school.

The Admiral served in Vietnam on a Patrol Boat, policing the Mekong Delta. [105] Following his two-year deployment, he cycled back to the United States, where he enrolled at the United States Naval Academy.

Admiral Carlson graduated as an officer, deploying multiple times around the globe. He advanced to the Joint Chiefs under the last administration. People within the military and outside it highly respected the Admiral.

George Dickens was a short, stocky man in his early sixties. He had short gray hair and spoke with a southern accent, having grown up in Alabama. He attended Auburn University and, subsequently, Yale Law School. The CIA recruited him. Nobody knew much about his career, as much of it was confidential.

Stan Perkins was the youngest of the ranking people in the room. He was in his mid-fifties. Stan grew up in the northern suburbs of Chicago, attended the University of Iowa, and returned to attend the University of Chicago School of Law. He immediately joined the FBI, served in multiple assignments in the field and at headquarters, and rose to his current position.

The other attendees were all younger, between thirty and mid-forties. Each was likely present because of their star status in their respective organizations.

Following the introductions, they sat around the expansive table. Casandra opened her laptop, preparing to record notes.

Gorge Dickens opened, "Thank you for coming here for such an urgent matter." He continued, "Lieutenant. Commander Murry, how is your wound?"

Jordan answered, "I am currently okay. The hand will be fine once I can get to a hospital to have it properly fixed."

George focused on Emma. "I understand you both have been on quite an adventure and a terrible ordeal. Please summarize your initial exploit and, most importantly, what you learned from your hostage experience?"

Emma responded, "Certainly."

She told her story, starting with her grandfather's revelation. She frequently looked at Jordan to add details.

Emma explained they had discovered Adolf Hitler and Eva Braun had escaped Germany, taking up residence in Bariloche as Adolf and Eve Schuttlemayer. They had a son, Dieter, and a grandson, Martin.

It took them almost twenty minutes to reach the point of being taken as hostages.

Emma said, "Dieter told us they had already inserted agents throughout the United States. Agents have crossed over our southern border for more than a year. They have resurrected Operation Pastorius and intend to blow up and destroy several targets throughout the United States.

They believe this will cause further unrest throughout our country, hopefully with more blame towards the Middle East. They intend to utilize this discord to initiate efforts to take over the country of Germany and once again bring the Nazi party to power."

Admiral Carlson asked, "Do you know anything regarding the targets?"

Emma confidently said, "Yes." She turned to Captain Freeman.

The captain removed a sheet of paper from his breast pocket. He said, "Here is a list of cities we discovered at the chalet. We believe these represent their planned target locations. He read the list: Boston, New York City, Atlanta, Dallas, Phoenix, San Francisco, Seattle, and Chicago."

"Anything else?" asked the Admiral.

"Yes, sir. We also received a potential identification of one of their assigned terrorists," he said as he presented the second sheet of paper.

The Admiral handed it to the technician. Casandra scanned the document using a portable device and projected it onto a large screen on the wall.

Collectively, the group studied the document. It included a photo of a man to be in his thirties, white, with a square jaw, small nose, mustache, blonde hair cut short, and round-rimmed glasses. The document listed his name as Max Harding and assigned him to Dallas. There was no other information and nothing about a specific target.

Dickens stated, "I think we can assume that there is at least one person assigned to each of the eight cities." All members nodded in agreement.

Stan Perkins said, "We should start our effort in trying to find this, Mr. Max Harding. I will contact our FBI office in Dallas and have a team immediately assigned to search for this suspect."

Dickens replied, "Yes, do that. What else can we do?"

Emma offered, "I am sure you have some facial recognition capabilities."

Dickens nodded, "Of course."

Emma added, "As you already know, I am a cybersecurity expert. I work for an innovative company that develops advanced facial recognition software. I think we should call them to inquire about using it."

Admiral Carlson commented, "I will make the call with you to reinforce that this is a national emergency and that it is urgent that they allow us to use the software."

Emma and Admiral Carlson left the room and entered an adjacent office. Emma placed the phone on speaker and dialed the direct number of her company CEO, Dan Landers.

"Hello, Dan Landers speaking."

Emma said, "Dan, this is Emma Miller-Murry. Time is critical. I am talking to you from the CIA Langley headquarters. Sitting here with me is the Secretary of the Navy, Admiral Carlson."

The Admiral said, "Hello, Mr. Landers. We urgently need access to your prototype facial recognition software."

Dan asked, "What is the problem?"

Admiral, "Because of national security, I cannot give you details. I can only say that this is a critical situation, and Emma tells us that your software will be quite useful to us in this matter."

Dan, "Emma, I certainly do not know what you have gotten yourself into, but I will authorize the Navy and CIA to use our software. I will email you authorization codes within the next fifteen minutes. You can use them to download the software and then access the application."

Emma and the Admiral simultaneously said. "Thank you."

Emma added, "Dan, thanks. This is a big help. Once this is all over, I will call to update you. I will watch for your email."

Emma and Admiral Carlson walked back to the conference room.

Emma announced, "We are getting permission to use the new software."

George asked, "What is so special about this software?"

Emma replied, "It operates at a much faster speed. It can search multiple locations simultaneously and has an application programming interface that connects with Artificial Intelligence, allowing it to compensate for potential physical disguises."

seven United States cities and your associates deployed there."

Max perked up a bit. He stated, "How do you know there are eight cities?"

The first agent replied, "A seal team found your bio and a list of eight United States target cities in a chalet in Bariloche, Argentina. Before the team's arrival, a group of Nazis, including Dieter Schuttlemayer and his son, Martin Schuttlemayer, held two Americans hostage and revealed to them the plans to deploy you and others to eight United States cities to execute terrorist activities."

Max said, "I cannot tell you anything."

The second agent said, "It would be in your best interest to tell us what you know. Otherwise, you will find yourself in an American solitary prison for years. We might even send you to Guantanamo Bay, never to be seen again."

Max leaned in, "If I tell you, they will kill me." He paused and looked at the two men, "I will only tell you if you give me a Presidential pardon, a new identity, placing me in your witness protection program, and enough money to live comfortably for the rest of my life."

First agent replied, "That's a pretty tall request."

Max retorted, "Take it or leave it."

The two agents left the room. They called Stan Perkins at Langley and informed him of their interrogation.

Stan responded, "We heard and watched everything on the monitor here. We will contact the President, brief him, and recommend accepting Max's request."

Stan turned to Admiral Carlson. "I think you should call the President."

The Admiral left the room. He wanted privacy when he spoke to the President.

Admiral Carlson dialed the phone. He had the direct number to the west wing office. He also knew the President was waiting there. They had previously briefed him on the situation.

Admiral Carlson stated, "Hello, Mr. President." He waited for the President's acknowledgment.

The Admiral continued, "Mr. President, we apprehended the primary suspect, Max Harding, and two of his associates in Dallas earlier today. Our FBI team in Dallas has interrogated the suspect.

We are certain that he is on a mission here for a renegade group of Nazis to carry-out terrorist acts in eight United States cities."

The Admiral paused and listened to the President.

Admiral Carlson stated, "The suspect will provide us details regarding the targets and his associates in return for a Presidential pardon, a new identity, placing him in our witness protection program, and providing him enough money to live comfortably for the rest of his life." He waited again for the President.

Admiral said, "Yes, Mr. President, we feel this quid pro quo is worth it. We must quickly apprehend these other suspects and eliminate the threat."

He listened to the President and stated, "Yes, we can also add a requirement that Max gives us information regarding the Schuttlemayers." He paused. "Thank you, Mr. President."

The Admiral returned to the main conference room and announced, "We have the President's approval to accept Max's request in return for information. The President will email a signed authorization form and letter to George within the next fifteen minutes."

George watched his email and waited for the documents. Once received, he forwarded it to Stan, who sent it to the agents at the Dallas FBI office.

The two FBI agents entered the interrogation room, confronting Max.

The first agent said, "Okay, Max, you have the President's approval." He then shoved the documents across the table at Max.

The second agent added, "These documents outline the President's basic approval regarding your demands. Later, we will provide the details regarding witness protection and funds to be delivered. We now want information regarding your associates, the targets, and the Schuttlemayers."

Now, just like the outcome of the original Operation Pastorius, one saboteur would divulge the identities of the other culprits. Max said, "Okay."

Max talked while the second agent wrote everything on a tablet. The second agent wrote the list of eight cities and scribed the target location next to each.

The Langley team watched, and Casandra also typed notes into her laptop.

Max provided the list. [107]

Boston—Faneuil Hall

New York City—The 911 Memorial

Atlanta—The College Football Hall of Fame

Dallas—The Texas School Book Depository Building

Phoenix—The Phoenix Zoo

San Francisco—Coit Tower

Seattle—Pike Place Market

Chicago—Navy Pier

The first agent then asked, "How many men at each, and what are their names?"

Max told them Dieter's plan required deploying three men at each city location. He gave the names of the team leaders for each, not knowing every man's name. He leaned back, smiling as if relieved he had betrayed his comrades.

The first agent said, "You are not done. We still need information about the Schuttlemayers."

Max leaned forward and calmly stated, "I know little more than you already know."

The first agent asked, "What about possible hiding locations for the Schuttlemayers? Other than the chalet we already discovered?"

Max thought for a brief moment and hesitated slightly. "There was another place in Argentina. It was higher in the mountains near Lago Steffen." [108]

The second agent opened his iPad and launched the Google Maps application. He typed Lago Steffen, Argentina. He turned the map screen towards Max and asked, "Show me where it is located."

Max used his fingers to zoom in on the map. He switched to satellite view. He scrolled the screen until he finally pointed. "There," he said.

The location was in a remote, wooded area south of Lago Steffen. The closest town was Rio Villegas.

Watching from Langley, Emma said to Stan, "Ask the agents to get descriptions of the city team leaders. We can use that in the new software. The AI interface can create a likely facial composite. We also will need Max to be available to help make identifications."

Stan phoned the agents in the room to tell them what Emma required.

Max described each city team leader. Emma entered those descriptions into the software.

Stan called the FBI office at each of the remaining seven cities. He provided a full briefing and instructions on deploying teams near each target location to begin surveillance.

George placed a call to a CIA Special Activities Center/Special Operations Group (SAC/SOG) team deployed in South America. They call upon these teams for tactical paramilitary operations. The CIA deploys the SOG teams for clandestine or covert operations in which the United States government does not want to be overtly associated with.

Many of the members of these units served in specialized United States military units like SEALS and Green Berets. George outlined their mission to breach the compound near Lago Steffen. Hopefully, they would apprehend the Schuttlemayers.

They would immediately travel to Rio Villegas. [109]

Emma walked across the room and hugged Jordan. She said, "I think we have this handled. You should go to the hospital and get treatment for your hand."

Jordan kissed her sweetly and said, "You are right, as usual." He turned to Admiral Carlson, holding up his injured hand, and asked, "Can I get some transportation to the hospital to get this hand treated?"

Admiral Carlson stated, "Certainly. I will order a car and driver to wait for you downstairs. He will take you to Walter Reed National Military Hospital, which is less than twenty minutes from here. I will also phone the hospital, informing them of your arrival. You will get the VIP treatment."

CHAPTER THIRTY-ONE
Snow White and the Seven Dwarfs

The Langley team watched the screen as the software compiled composites for the seven city team leaders. As it completed one, it populated the screen tiles with a facial image. It took nearly thirty minutes to display all seven.

George and Stan had already designated the capture operation as Snow White and the Seven Dwarfs. Dieter Schuttlemayer, dubbed Snow White, and the city team leaders were each assigned the names of one of the seven dwarfs. Their monikers were Boston - Happy, New York City - Doc, Atlanta - Grumpy, Phoenix - Dopey, San Francisco - Bashful, Seattle - Sleepy, and Chicago - Sneezy. [110]

The respective tiles on the screen tagged a name associated with each. For an added touch, they designated Martin Schuttlemayer as Br'er Rabbit. [111]

Casandra electronically sent the images to the Dallas FBI agents. They showed the facial composites to Max. He suggested changes to all seven.

She received the modifications and, along with Emma, input those into the software. The large screen showed seven final composites.

Casandra sent each of the seven images to the respective FBI field team in the seven target cities.

There was nothing more for the Langley team to do. They now needed to wait.

Later that day, they received word from the South American SOG team leader, Sam Rivers. Sam reported that they have assembled the team in Buenos Aires. It comprised four SOG agents and a twelve-member SEAL team led by Captain Freeman. They would travel overnight to reach Rio Villegas. There, they would rest and reconnoiter the mountain home, allowing them to make final plans for an assault the following day.

George had already worked through channels to inform the Argentine government that an American team was in their country for an operation. He provided some general parameters, but nothing specific. They needed to maintain secrecy, as they did not know what information might get passed to the Schuttlemayers. They needed to keep the Argentine police out of this operation.

Shortly following Sam's check-in, the Langley team received reports from each of the seven city FBI teams. All advised that they had agents deployed at each target location. They also stated that they had not yet seen their suspect but were keeping an alert for such.

Emma diligently worked on the facial recognition software, hoping to catch an identification of the suspects.

It was late in the evening. The Langley team was exhausted, and they needed rest to remain sharp. They worked through the night in two teams, in three-hour shifts. One team would remain working in the conference room, while the other team slept in sleeping quarters on the second floor of the CIA headquarters building.

The FBI assigned Emma and Casandra to separate teams. They possessed the technical skills needed to monitor the software and other communications. Admiral Carlson and George joined separate teams, with the Admiral assigned to Emma. The group set Stan with George.

The FBI agent Beth split from Kevin, with Kevin posted to Emma and CIA agent Kelsey divided from Scott, with Kelsey assigned alongside Emma.

The air smelled of fresh pine and early morning dew. There was a faint smell of burning wood wafting from the enormous fireplace atop the mountain house roof.

The group watched as the assault teams approached from all four directions. Their movements appeared like a choreographed ballet performance.

Captain Freeman, leading assault team one, reached the front entrance on the north side after silently downing one perimeter guard and removing two guards outside the entrance.

Sam Rivers, working with assault team three, gained access to the rear door after killing one guard patrolling the outer area and a second guard at the door.

Assault team two approached from the east side. They knifed two perimeter guards before reaching the house wall. The last group, assault team four, reached the west side wall after successfully downing two perimeter guards.

Captain Freeman announced over his microphone, "All assault teams confirm your positions."

Each team responded,

"Assault team two, in position at the east wall."

"Assault team three, in position at the rear door."

"Assault team four, in position on the west wall."

Captain Freeman gave the order, "Breach."

The front and rear teams blew the doors open using C4 explosives. All eight members rushed inside the house. Two members from team two remained at the east wall, while the other two moved respectively to the front and rear areas. Assault team four performed this same maneuver. Their deployment created guarding positions from the rear and handled anyone who might try to leave out the door.

They heard gunfire from inside the house. Meanwhile, three guards stormed toward the front entrance. The two

SEAL team members, hiding behind bushes, opened fire on the charging men. The SEALS rapidly removed the attackers.

Six additional guards attacked from the west side. They had been sleeping in a nearby building, later determined to be a small bunkhouse. It took the team longer to conceal there completely to thwart the attack.

Four guards exited the house through the rear door. Team three positioned there instantly killed three men. A fourth ran around the corner to the east side where team two waiting there easily killed that guard.

It took fifteen minutes to complete the assault. Captain Freeman and Sam Rivers exited the front entrance, and the other team members escorted their prisoners.

Captain Freeman ordered his teams to all gather in the front yard. Each team reported on the number of guards killed and no injuries to any team member. The captain reported both inside teams were uninjured and that they killed the remaining four guards inside the house.

Pointing at the prisoners, Captain Freeman announced loud enough for the Langley team to hear, "We have secured the premises. We killed twenty-four guards. We have five prisoners. One is Snow White. The other four are the butler, chef, maid, and a house servant."

The Langley team all cheered at the success of the mission.

George asked, "What about Br'er Rabbit?"

"No sign of him," replied Freeman.

George ordered, "Sam, you should immediately question Snow White."

Sam deliberately moved to face Dieter. He asked, "Where is your son?"

Dieter coughed and placed his hand in front of his mouth. Within ten seconds, white foam appeared, flowing from his mouth like lava from a volcano. His legs buckled, and his body dropped to the ground. He had consumed poison.

The faces of the Langley team showed complete shock.

It shocked George that nobody had searched the prisoners and that the team had failed to secure their hands.

As Dieter lay motionless on the ground, the butler said, "I can give you some input on Martin Schuttlemayer's whereabouts." All heads craned towards the butler, who added, "Of course, I will want preferential treatment for telling you such information."

Admiral Carlson loudly said over the speaker, "Captain, you give the butler assurance we will not detain him, and we will reward him if he provides information about the location of Br'er Rabbit."

Captain Freeman relayed this commitment to the butler.

The butler nodded and told the Captain that Martin Schuttlemayer departed two days ago and headed to Montevideo, Uruguay.

Hearing this, George ordered Sam to assist Captain Freeman in maintaining the security of the compound and searching it for any further information.

Meanwhile, he would deploy another CIA team to Montevideo.

CHAPTER THIRTY-FOUR

Chasing Br'er Rabbit

The second CIA team, led by Joe Bridgers, arrived in Montevideo from Miami. Three field agents accompanied him.

Joe had already received information from Emma that the facial recognition software had located Br'er Rabbit at a hotel in Montevideo. Emma had received a photo of Martin, obtained by Sam, upon searching the mountain home, and she uploaded that to the software.

Joe's team, accompanied by local police and an Interpol agent, entered the hotel lobby and inquired at the desk about Martin Schuttlemayer. The desk clerk informed them that Mr. Schuttlemayer was in room 612 on the hotel's sixth floor.

Joe, the Interpol inspector, and the local police lieutenant went up the elevator to the sixth floor. Joe ordered two men to remain in the lobby and the other two to go up the stairs to guard that escape route.

Once everyone was in position, Joe and his two colleagues knocked on the door to room 612. Nobody answered, so Joe used the master key provided by the desk clerk to open the door. They entered the room with guns drawn, fully prepared to protect themselves. The room was empty.

Tom communicated these findings to Stan, who relayed it all to the Langley team. After discussion amongst the team, Stan was to call Tom, giving him instructions regarding the prisoners. Stan told Tom to release the three people deemed associates of the primary suspect. They had done nothing to which the FBI would charge them.

He ordered Tom to arrest Martin Schuttlemayer formally. Stan told Tom to take Martin to the local police jail, after which the FBI will transport Martin to Washington, DC., where they will charge him, and he will proceed to trial.

Admiral Carlson contacted the President, providing a full briefing. The President thanked the Admiral and the entire Langley team. He expressly asked Admiral Carlson to thank Emma and Jordan for their involvement from the beginning. Their efforts saved many American lives and helped uncover and dissolve an evil organization.

The Admiral conveyed the President's thanks and praise to the Langley team. They gave each other a high-five and congratulations. Emma beamed with pride.

CHAPTER THIRTY-FIVE
Rendezvous with Jordan

Emma sat in the hospital chair in Jordan's room, waiting for him to wake. She thought about how wonderful it was to be at his side and how fortunate they both were to be okay now with the ordeal finished.

Jordan awakened from his slumber. He rolled his head towards Emm, his eyes wide open, and smiled. He said, "Good morning. It's nice to see you."

Emm moved to sit on his bed. Holding his good hand, she replied, "I am so glad to be here with you now." She leaned down and kissed him passionately.

Jordan pressed the remote button, raising his torso to an upright position. He was eager to soak in Emm's companionship.

Emm briefed Jordan on the complete activities of the Langley team during the past couple of days. She filled him in on the details of each field team's execution of Operation Snow White and the Seven Dwarfs. Emma explained how Dieter Schuttlemayer took poison upon capture. She provided explicit facts about the capture of Martin Schuttlemayer and specifically noted that he, unlike his father, was too chicken to take his own life.

Jordan commented, "It sounds exhilarating." He paused, grinned at her, and stated, "It sounds like you had a key role in the effort."

CHAPTER THIRTY-SIX
Home in Eastport

Emma and Jordan pulled into their driveway in Eastport. It was a less than one-hour drive from Walter Reed Hospital. Which was good, because Jordan would need to return there for additional surgery and treatment over the next year.

The sun shined brightly in mid-morning. The sky displayed a beautiful robin egg blue accented with giant puffy white clouds.

It had been quite a few weeks since they last saw their quaint cottage home. They had arranged for landscaping service, and the yard looked well-maintained. It was odd that the flags were hanging from the front porch posts. They removed the flags during their last visit home. Perhaps a neighbor placed the flags in their holders.

They shut off the engine and exited the vehicle. Troy and Janessa surprised them as they raced through the front entrance while she and Jordan walked toward the porch. Troy knew where they had hidden the spare key, which he used for access to the house. Undoubtedly, they erected the flags.

Troy shouted from the porch, "Hello!" He then saluted them and added, "Good to see you home, Captains." He had already heard the good news about their promotions.

Emma ran to Troy, standing in the front yard, giving him a friendly hug. She pulled back and said, "I've not yet decided to accept the return to active duty."

Troy replied, "You will."

Jordan interrupted. "Thanks for being here. It's great to see you."

Troy grinned and said, "We wanted to give you a welcome home surprise."

Jordan said, "Your presence is indeed a surprise. It is always good to see you."

Troy responded, "We have a lot to catch up on. You two had quite an ordeal after we departed the Canary Islands."

"Yes, we did," said Jordan. He squeezed Emm's hand. "We have one heck of a story to tell you," he added.

Troy smiled and said, "You can give us the full details over a cold beer waiting inside. Meanwhile, I have some news for you."

Troy turned, motioning for Janessa, still standing on the porch, to join him at his side. Janessa bounded to Troy's side, beaming a radiant smile. Once there, Troy wrapped his arm around her waist. He announced, "We have something to tell you both." He looked at their faces. Both Emma and Jordan looked puzzled and anxious. Troy continued, "We are getting married."

Emma leaped forward, hugging Janessa, and shouted, "Congratulations!"

Extending his good hand, Jordan reached out to shake Troy's hand and wrapped his other arm around Troy's neck, embracing him tightly. He said, "Good for you both." Jordan added, "I was beginning to think you would be a permanent bachelor. I am glad you found your soulmate."

Jordan directed his attention towards Janessa, wrapping her in an affectionate hug. He said, "Congratulations. I am so happy for you both."

Similarly, Emma embraced Troy and said, "It's about time you settle down." She then stepped away, hugging her husband and said, "I wish you both the same joy that we share."

Janessa held out her hand to display the diamond engagement ring. Emma saw that the ring displayed its beautiful one-carat Asscher-shaped diamond set in white gold. The stone shimmered brilliantly in the sunlight. The diamond featured a square shape with cut corners and step cuts, making it uniquely chic in a temporary setting while also perfectly complementing vintage styles.

Emma excitedly commented, "That is beautiful."

Jordan added, "Let's get the car unpacked and celebrate."

The foursome carried luggage inside. The group wasted little time celebrating. Troy previously placed a bottle of Veuve Clicquot Brut Yellow Label Champaign in an ice bucket, and it was ready to drink. Troy popped the cork and poured four glasses of the chilled bubbly beverage.

They toasted and cheered. They swiftly consumed the first pouring. Troy emptied the bottle and filled the four glasses.

Following the engagement congratulations revelry, Jordan and Emma told the story of their adventure after leaving the Canary Islands. They provided details about their hostage experience and the ensuing teamwork, thwarting the terrorist plan of the new Nazis.

Their storytelling time exceeded the time needed to consume a single bottle of Champaign. Emma prepared a pitcher of margaritas to supplement the first beverage.

They finished the second pitcher of margaritas. Emma said, "We are all out of margaritas, and we have not fully stocked the house for a party. This celebration calls for McGarvey's."

The other three cheered and said, "Great idea. Let's go."

The foursome walked the twenty minutes. They knew a big celebration would mean not driving home, and it also took some work to find parking near Dock Street. Before leaving the house, they opened a bottle of red wine previously stored in a cabinet. Jordan poured the red liquid in Styrofoam cups from which they drank en route to the bar.

Jordan held open the door and said, "Here we are."

They pushed through the crowd, making their way quickly to the back bar. Skip, the bartender, greeted them heartily, "Hello. It's good to have you back." He paused and asked, "What will you have?"

Jordan answered, "Four coffee shooters to start."

Following consumption of the specialty drinks, Troy ordered a bottle of the Moet & Chandon Imperial Brut Champagne.

Skip retrieved the bottle, popped the cork, and served four glasses. He asked, "What is the celebration?"

Janessa, holding Troy's hand with her right hand, held out her left hand, showing the diamond engagement ring. She shouted, "We are engaged to be married!"

The foursome clinked their glasses and sipped the bubbly liquid. The carbon dioxide gas bubbles bounce on their noses.

Troy shouted to Skip, "Yes, we are celebrating our engagement, and Jordan is being promoted to captain."

Jordan hesitated and looked at Emm. He said, "Are we celebrating for you as well?"

Emma grinned and replied, "Yes, I will be returning to active duty."

Jordan grabbed her hand and raised their arms. He shouted, "My wonderful wife is returning to active duty as a Navy Captain!"

Skip announced, "Coffee shooters for everyone."

BIBLIOGRAPHY

Cosmopolitan. n.d.
https://cosmoploitan.com/lifestyle/a39304449/666-angel-number-meaning-numerology/ (accessed December 2023).

Anil K. Jain, Yi Chen, and Meltem Demirkus. "Pores and Ridges: high resolution fingerprint matching using level 3 features." January 2007.
https://www.semanticscholar.org/paper/Pores-and-Ridges%3A-High_Resolution-Fingerprint-Using_Jain-Chen/a4bc8a05aafc549cab0e2ddc3002828232bec1d5f0 (accessed October 2023).

Anti Defamation League. *88/Hate Symbolism Database.* n.d.
https://adl.org/resources/hate-symbolism/88 (accessed December 2023).

Austin, We Are. *Wurst is Almost Here! Do You Know the Origin of the Chicken Dance?* November 3, 2022.
https://cbsaustin.com (accessed February 27, 2024).

Barton, eric. *Where to Celebrate Oktoberfest in the US.* September 8, 2023. https://www.timeout.com (accessed February 27, 2024).

Bianchi, Saabastian. "Documents: Documents of the Wehrmacht." *Documents of the Wehrmacht.* n.d.
https://wehrmacht-awards.com/documents/wehrpass.htm (accessed October 2023).

Stanska, Zuzzana. "10 Most Important Masterpieces Lost During World War II." *Daily Art Magazine.* June 1, 2023. https://www.dailyartmagazine.com/10-important-masterpieces-lost-ii-world-war/#:~:text=1.,Czartoryski%20Museum%2C%20Krakow%2C%20Poland. (accessed August 2023).

"Swiss Wine." *Wine Searcher.* n.d. https://www.wine-searcher.com/regions-switzerland (accessed October 2023).

Tabb, Kip. "When World War II Was On the Outer Banks." *Coastal Review.* July 17, 2020. https://coastalrevview.org/2020/07/when-wwii-was-on-the-outer-banks/ (accessed August 2023).

The Library of Congress. *The Germans in America.* April 23, 2014. https://www.loc,gov/rr/european/imde/germchro.html# (accessed February 27, 2024).

"The Nazi Party: The Abwehr." *The National Jewish Library.* n.d. https://jewishvirtuallibrary.org/the-abwehr (accessed August 2023).

"The Wolfpacks-German U-Boats Operations-Kriegsmarine." *uboat.net.* n.d. https://uboat.net/ops/wolfpacks/overview.htm (accessed December 2023).

"Torpedo Junction." *National Parks Service.* September 28, 2016. https://nps.gov/articles/wwii_caha_torpedo_junction.htm (accessed August 2023).

UC Santa Barbara. "Proclamation 2561-Denying Certain Enemies Access to the Courts." *The Amercan Presidency Project.* n.d. https://www.presidency.ucsb.edu (accessed August 2023).

—. "Remarks at the Rathaus in Cologne After Signing the Golden Book." *The Amercan Presidency Project.* n.d. https://presidency.ucsb.edu/documents/remarks-the-

rathaus-cologne-after-signing-the-golden-book#
(accessed October 2023).

US Army Center of Military History. n.d.
https://history.army.mil/brochures/rhineland/rhineland.
ht (accessed October 2023).

US Naval Academy. *USNA Sailing Center.* n.d.
https://usna.edu/sailing/index.php (accessed July 2023).

VA-US Dept of Veterans Affairs. *National Cemetery Administration.* n.d.
https://www.va.gov/cems/nchp/hampton.asp (accessed October 2023).

Villa Winter Cofete. 2023. https://casa.wintercofete.com/en/
(accessed December 2023).

What are three positive integers whose sum equals their product. n.d.
https://algebra.com/algebra/homework/word/numbers/
Number_Word_Problems_faq.question (accessed December 2023).

Whealey, Robert H. "Hitler and Spain: The Nazi Role in the Spanish Civil War, 1936-1939." *The University Press of Kentucky.* n.d.
https://ukknowledge.uky.edu/upk_european_history/5
(accessed December 2023).

Wikipedia. *666.* December 2023.
https://en.wikipedia.org/wiki/666_(numbers) (accessed December 2023).

Abwehr. September 11, 2023.
https://en.wikipedia.or/wiki/Abwehr (accessed September 2023).

Argentina during WWII. August 8, 2023.
https://en.wikipedia.org/wiki/Argentina_during_world_
War_II (accessed August 2023).

Bariloche. November 9, 2023.
      https://en.wikipedia.org/wiki/Barilcohe (accessed
      November 2023).

Basel. December 11, 2023. https://en.wikipedia.org/wiki/Basel
      (accessed December 2023).

Battle of Cologne (1945). December 3, 2023.
      https://en.wikipedia.org/wiki/Battle_of_Cologne_(1945)
      (accessed December 2023).

Bombing of Cologne. June 25, 2023.
      https://en.wikipedia.org/wiki/Bombing_of_Cologne_in_
      World_War_ii (accessed June 2023).

Buenos Aires. December 12, 2023.
      https://en.wikipedia.org/wiki/Buenos_Aires (accessed
      December 2023).

Cologne. December 17, 2023.
      https://en.wikipedia.org/wiki/Cologne (accessed
      December 2023).

Cologne Cathedral. September 25, 2023.
      https://en.wikipedia.org/wiki/Cologne_Cathedral
      (accessed September 2023).

Cologne Cathedral. December 14, 2023.
      https://en.wikipedia.org/wiki/Cologne_Cathedral
      (accessed December 2023).

Conspiracy theories about Adolf Hitler's death. October 9, 2023.
      https://en.wikipedia.org/wiki/Conspiracy_theories_about
      _Adolf_Hitler%27s_death (accessed October 2023).

Death of Adolf Hitler. October 8, 2023.
      https://en.wikipedia.org/wiki/Death_of_Adolf_Hitler
      (accessed October 2023).

Dog Tag. September 9, 2023. https://en.wikipedia.org/wiki/Dog-
      tag (accessed September 2023).

EL-DE Haus. February 9, 2022. https://en.wikipedia.org/wiki/EL-
      DE_Haus (accessed December 2023).

Estrella Damm. n.d. https://en.wikipedia.org/wiki/Estrella_Damm (accessed December 2023).

Fuerteventura. December 11, 2023. https://en.wikipedia.org/wiki/Fuerteventura (accessed December 2023).

German submarine U-202. December 3, 2023. https://en.wikipedia.org/wiki/German_submarine_U-202 (accessed December 2023).

German submarine U-530. December 17, 2023. https://en.wikipedia.org/wiki/German_submarine_U-530 (accessed December 2023).

German submarine U-707. June 7, 2023. https://en.wikipediae.org/wiki/German_submarine_U-707 (accessed June 2023).

German Submarine U-85 (1941). August 24, 2023. https://en.wikipedia.org/wiki/German_submarine_U-85_(1941) (accessed August 2023).

German submarine U-977. December 14, 2023. https://en.wikipedia.org/wiki/German_submarine_U-977 (accessed December 2023).

German submarineU-584. September 3, 2023. https://en.wikipedai.org/wiki/German_submarine_U-584 (accessed September 2023).

Gibraltar. November 20, 2023. https://en.wikipedia.org/wiki/Gibraltar (accessed November 2023).

Hampton National Cemetery. February 12, 2023. https://en.wikipedia.org/wiki/Hampton_National_Cemetery (accessed February 2023).

Josef Frings. May 23, 2023. https://en.wikipedia.org/wiki/Josef_Frings (accessed May 2023).

Karl Dönitz. September 18, 2023.
  https://en.wikipedia.org/wiki/Karl_Dönitz (accessed
  September 2023).

Lanzarote. December 17, 2023.
  https://en.wikipedia.org/wiki/Lanzarote (accessed
  December 2023).

List of Wolfpacks of World War II. January 7, 2023.
  https://en.wikipedia.org/wiki/List_of_wolfpacks_of_Worl
  d_War_II (accessed December 2023).

Munich. December 14, 2023.
  https://en.eikipedia.org/wiki/Munich (accessed
  December 2023).

Navy 44 (M&R). January 30, 2023.
  https://en.wikipedia.org/wiki/Navy_44_(M%26R)
  (accessed February 2023).

Nazi Plunder. September 24, 2023.
  https://en.wikipedia.org/wiki/Nazi_plunder#:~:text=With
  %20the%20looted%20degenerate%20art,of%20Gabrielle
  %20Diot%20by%20Degas. (accessed September 2023).

Operation Pastorius. September 14, 2023.
  htpps://en.wikipedia.org/wiki/Operation_Pastorius
  (accessed September 2023).

Otto Müller. January 25, 2022.
  https://en.wikipedia.org/wiki/Otto_M%C3%BCller_(pries
  t) (accessed February 2022).

Portrait of a Young Man (Raphael). n.d.
  https://en.wikipedia.org/wiki/Portrait+of_a_Young_Man
  _(Raphael) (accessed December 2023).

Ratlines (WWII). December 17, 2023.
  https://en.wikipedia.org/wiki/Ratlines_(World_War_II)
  (accessed December 2023).

Resuplly of German submarines in Spain, 1940-1944. December
  21, 2022.

https://en.wikipedia.org/wiki/resupply_of_German_sub
marines_in_Spain,_1940-1944 (accessed December
2022).

Rocky Mount, North Carolina. July 18, 2023.
https://en.wikipedia.org/wiki/Rocky_Mount_North_Carol
ina (accessed August 2023).

Siegestor. September 18, 2023.
https://en.wikipedia.org/wiki/Siegestor (accessed
September 2023).

United States Naval Academy. September 12, 2023.
https://en.wikipedia.org/wiki/United_States_Naval_Acad
emy (accessed September 2023).

Villa Winter. Novemnber 2, 2021.
https://en.wikipedia.org/wiki/Villa_Winter (accessed
October 2023).

Wilhelm Canaris. August 30, 2023.
https://en.wikipedia.org/wiki/Wilhelm_Canaris (accessed
September 2023).

Wolfpack (naval tactic). December 19, 2023.
https://en.wikipedia.org/wiki/Wolfpack_(naval_tactic)
(accessed December 2023).

"Wilhelm Canaris." *The National Jewish Library.* n.d.
https://jewishvirtuallibrary.org/wilhelm-canaris
(accessed September 2023).

William, Chris. "The Wehrpass." *Military Trader.* November 12,
2019. https://militarytrader.com/militaria-
collectibles/the-wehrpass (accessed October 2023).

INDEX

ENDNOTES

1. The Navy built the Navy 44 for US Naval Academy sailing training in 1985.
2. Robert Crown Sailing Center is the name of the sailing center at the US Naval Academy.
3. McGarvey's is an Irish pub in Annapolis, near the dock, and just outside the US Naval Academy.
4. Monterey, California, is the location for US Naval Academy postgraduate work.
5. All three ships and classes were operational in the U.S. Navy at the time of writing.
6. The 80 train carried passengers to Philadelphia for medical treatment.
7. The Atlantic Coast Line RR did make its northern headquarters in Rocky Mount, NC.
8. 4F was a means of designating men/women unfit for military service during WWII.
9. Our Lady of Perpetual Hope Catholic Church was authorized in 1939 and is still in operation.
10. Pineview Cemetery is located just outside downtown Rocky Mount, NC.
11. Psalm 23: The Good Shepherd uses the words from the NSRV Catholic Version.
12. The Abwehr was a German intelligence-gathering agency formed before WWII and operated throughout the war.
13. OKW was the supreme military command and control of Nazi Germany during WWII.
14. Wilhelm Canaris (January 1887- April 1945) was a German admiral and the chief of the Abwehr from 1935 to 1944.

15. Adolf Hitler (April 1889 - April 1945) was an Austrian- born German politician who rose to power as the leader of the Nazi party, becoming chancellor in 1933 and the title of Fuhrer in 1934. He led Germany into and through WWII until his death in April 1945. In 1945, he married his longtime companion Eva Braun (Feb 1912 – April 1945); she also died with him in 1945.

16. On September 1, 1939, Germany attacked The Polish military depot at Westerplatte, starting WWII.

17. Quenz Lake is located in Brandenburg, Germany; during WWII, a converted mansion on the lake served as a training ground for spies.

18. Operation Pastorius was a failed German intelligence plan for sabotage inside the USA during WWII.

19. The Geneva Convention is international humanitarian law. Two treaties existed following 1929, one dealing with the 'treatment of prisoners'; these two treaties were updated after WWII, and two additional ones were added.

20. Lt. Eberhard Gregor (Sept 1915 – Apr 1942) was assigned command of the German submarine U-85 on June 7, 1941.

21. The three freighters sunk by U-85 are all documented; the ships sunk by all U-boats in 1942 are all documented; the Germans often referred to this as the Atlantic Turkey Shoot.

22. Operation Drumroll (Drumbeat) was a German submarine operation conceived by Karl Dönitz. He deployed five long-range submarines to the Atlantic seaboard to disrupt and sink merchant ships traveling from Maine to Texas. They enjoyed success from January 1942 to August 1942.

23. Historical records document that the U-85 sank the Christina Knudsen.

24. USS Roper was the first U.S. Navy ship to sink a German submarine in WWII.

25. Lt. Cmd. Hamilton W. Howe, captain of the USS Roper, sank the U-85 on April 13/14, 1942, and the Navy awarded him the Navy Cross.

26. The US government buried twenty-nine sailors from U-85 in Hampton National Cemetery, Hampton, Virginia, with military honors on the evening of April 15, 1942. Fifty-two prisoners from Fort Monroe prepared and later filled the graves.

27. From 1942 to 1945, there was a radar installation in Kitty Hawk.

28. German submarine U-202 participated in Operation Pastorius, landing at Amagansett, Long Island, NY, on June 13, 1942, with the German Adwehr agents Dasch, Burger, Guirin, and Heiick; they did encounter U.S. Coastguardsman John Cullen.

29. U-202 did run aground but managed to escape before being captured.

30. German submarine U-584 did participate in Operation Pastorius and surface at Ponte Vedra Beach, Florida, on June 18, 1942, landing the Abwehr agents Kerling, Haupt, Neubauer, & Thiel.

31. Dasch and Burger did hatch a plan to betray the other six Abwehr agents. They contacted the FBI and worked with D. M. Ladd.

32. President Roosevelt issued an Executive Proclamation on July 2, 1942, essentially establishing the Abwehr agents' trial in military court rather than a civil hearing.

33. Lauson Stone and Kenneth Royall represented the Abwehr agents. Still, they were unsuccessful in moving the trial to a civil court.

34. Six of the eight Abwehr agents were found guilty and executed on August 8, 11942; they sentenced Dasch and Burger to life in prison.

35. In 1948, President Truman granted Executive Clemency to Dasch and Burger.

36. On April 15, 1942, the US military buried the 29 sailors of U-85 with full military honors at night. Fifty-two prisoners from Fort Morgan prepared and filled the graves.

37. The government established new headstones for the U-85 sailors on November 14, 2004.

38. Boatyard Bar and Grill is located in Annapolis, Maryland, in the historic maritime district of Eastport.

39. Riverwalk Landings Piers is located in Yorktown, Virginia.

40. Water Street Grille is located in Yorktown, VA.

41. Erich Degenkolb, one of the sailors killed on the German submarine U-85, is buried at the Hampton National Phoebus Cemetery in row P, grave number 694.

42. Soldbuch was the personal identification book the German Army gave each German soldier.

43. The German Army only issued one 'dog tag' perforated in the middle for soldier identification; the US military issued two 'dog tags' to each soldier.

44. Wehrpass was personal identification issued to every German citizen during WWII; each soldier turned that in and was given a Soldbuch upon entering the military.

45. Davis Pub is located in Eastport, Maryland.

46. Marienplatz is a central square in Munich, Germany.

47. Bayerischer Hof Hotel, located in the heart of Munich, Germany, is an excellent luxury property.

48. Hofbräuhaus is a famous beer hall restaurant located in Munich, Germany.

49. AIFS is a recognized fingerprint identification process.

50. Siegestor is a three-arched memorial arch in Munich, Germany. King Ludwig of Bavaria commissioned it and completed it in 1852. It is dedicated to the glory of the Bavarian army. Today, it is a monument and reminder of peace.

51. Restaurant Tantris is located in Munich, Germany.

52. This excerpt is a copy of the Oath of Office (officer version) used by the United States Navy.

53. There is a mathematical theory that the square of any odd integer minus 1 is divisible by 8.

54. Cologne Cathedral is the tallest twin-spired church in the world; initially built in 1248-1560, Germany's most visited landmark is located in Cologne, Germany; there is no recorded history of hiding Nazi treasure there.

55. Dr. Emanuel Schäfer, Franz Sprinz, and Kurt Matschke were two Gestapo leaders stationed at the Cologne Gestapo building a few blocks from Cologne Cathedral during WWII; Archbishop Josef Frings (February 6, 1887 – December 17, 1978) served as Archbishop of Cologne from 1942 to 1969.

56. The Germans did control the Rhine River until early 1945. From March 5 to March 7, 145, the Allies executed Operation Lumberjack, seizing control of Cologne, Germany. A famous tank battle took place outside the Cathedral.

57. These seven paintings and three others are listed as the ten most essential masterpieces lost during WWII.

58. Breslauer Platz is a small roundabout in Cologne. In the center stands an Obelisk of Tutankhamun by American artist Rita McBride, erected on July 7, 2017.

59. Peters Brauhaus is a famous German restaurant in Cologne, Germany.

60. The listed artifacts are on-site at the Cologne Cathedral.

61. The Shrine of the Three Kings, on exhibit in the Cologne Cathedral, is a large gilded and decorated triple sarcophagus built between 1180 and 1225. It is traditionally believed to hold the bones of the Biblical Magi.

62. Otto Müller (1870-1944) was a German Roman Catholic priest active in the resistance movement against Adolph Hitler; he was implicated in the July plot, Operation Valkyrie, to kill Hitler; he died in custody. The Müller family name used in this story is unrelated to Otto Müller.

63. Allied Operation Lumberjack, which took place from March 5 to March 7, 1945, successfully seized control of Cologne; a tank battalion occurred on March 6 outside the Cathedral.

64. Otto Doppelfeld (1907-1979) was a German archaeologist and prehistorian. He led the effort to excavate and repair the Cologne Cathedral after WWII. Still, he did not find any secret rooms or treasures.

65. Gaffel am Dom is an establishment near Cologne Cathedral serving Gaffel Kölsch.

66. German Purity Law of 1516 established strict requirements for brewing Kölsch beer.

67. Brauhaus Früh am Dom is an establishment near Cologne Cathedral serving Früh Kölsch beer.

68. Basel is a city on the Rhine River in Switzerland. De-Wette Park is located across the street from the Hilton Hotel.

69. Basel Minster, built 1019 – 1500, is a Romanesque and Gothic cathedral in Old Basel. It was initially a Catholic cathedral and is now a Reformed Protestant church.

70. Walliser Kane Restaurant is a Swiss cuisine restaurant in Basel, Switzerland.

71. Pythagoras was a Greek who thrived during the 6th century BC. Pythagorean assigned specific numbers with mystic properties.

72. The Biblical meaning of 666 can be a reference to The Beast.

73. The number 666 is considered an Angel number, meaning balance, harmony, and focus.

74. The number 666 is the sum of the first thirty-six natural numbers, which makes it a triangular number.

75. Gustav Winter (May 1893 – November 1971) was a German engineer who in 1937 received funding from Marshal Herman Göring's German department to build Casa Winter on the island of Fuerteventura.

76. The Etappendienst was a secret German U-boat supply operation reestablished by Admiral Canaris to supply U-boats during WWII. There are 25 cases of U-boats secretly supplied in Spanish ports, including the Canary Islands. Kurt Meyer-Döhner was the German naval attaché in Spain during WWII.

77. Tempelhof Airport was constructed in Berlin 1936-1941; there are recorded findings of a tunnel system connecting the Fuher's bunker with the airport; there was a mass exodus of Nazis from Tempelhof Airport on April 2, 1945.

78. German submarine U-977 surrendered in Mar del Plata, Argentina, on August 17, 1945; there is a record of it stopping at Cape Verde islands.

79. San Carlos de Bariloche is a mountain town in the Patagonia region of Argentina. Before WWII, many Germans from Germany, Austria, and Slovenia settled here; after WWII, several Nazis fled Germany to South America, with some making their way to Bariloche.

80. Juan Peron (1895 – 1974) served as President of Argentina for two terms, June 1946 – Sept 1955 and Oct 1973 – July 1944; he was a known sympathizer to the Nazis. Ratline is a term associated with the escape route of Nazis to Argentina after WWII; the Nazis listed did escape Germany; Erich Priebke was discovered in Bariloche, Argentina, in 1994.

81. German submarine U-530 surrendered at Mar del Plata, Argentina, on July 10, 1945.

82. E L & N is a restaurant in the London airport.

83. Lanzarote Marina is on the island of Lanzarote, part of the Canary Islands chain; Puerto de Morro Jabal is a marina on Fuerteventura, another Canary Island.

84. There are recorded instances of Orcas attacking or interfering with boats near the Iberian Peninsula, the Mediterranean Sea, and the Straights of Gibraltar.

85. Arrecife is one of the main towns on the island of Lanzarote.

86. NAO, Bermeja, and Rote are three breweries currently operating on Lanzarote.

87. Barbacana Bar and Grill is a restaurant operating in Arrecife, Lanzarote.

88. El Grifo Winery has been operating on Lanzarote since 1775.

89. Cofete is a small village town on the road to Casa Winter on the Fuerteventura Island.

90. The eight lunar phases of the moon are new moon, waxing crescent, first quarter, waxing gibbous, full moon, waning gibbous, third quarter, and waning crescent: the cycle repeats once a month (every 29.5 days).

91. The number 88 is a white supremacist numerical code for "Heil Hitler"; H is the eighth letter of the alphabet, so 88 = HH = Heil Hitler.

92. Restaurant Cofete Pepe El Faro operates in the village of Cofete on Fuerteventura Island.

93. Estrella Damm is a lager beer brewed in Barcelona, Spain, since 1876. August Küntzmann Damm initially brewed the beer.

94. In 1954, Phillip Citroen, a former SS officer, approached the CIA, providing a photo of him and a man named Adolf Schuttlemayer, alleged to be Adolf Hitler. He claimed Hitler was living in Tunja, Columbia, north of Bogota. Another CIA contact, code-named CIMELODY-3, conveyed the same story. Adolf Schuttlemayer fled to somewhere in Argentina in 1955.

95. Market Square Coffee Shop operates in Fuerteventura airport.

96. Goethe Bar and Grill operates in Frankfurt airport.

97. Hotel Plaza Central Canning is a hotel operating in the Canning district of Buenos Aires, Argentina.

98. Scandinavian Outdoor Shop is a retail store in Buenos Aires, Argentina's Los Toscas Plaza district.

99. Charming Luxury Lodge and Private Spa is a high-end lodge and restaurant on Lake Huapi, on the outskirts of Bariloche, Argentina.

100. Cerro Catedral Ski Resort is a main ski resort operating near Bariloche, Argentina.

101. Cathedral, Our Lady of Nahuel Huapi, is the primary Catholic Church in Bariloche, Argentina, built in 1942-1944. It sits in a park located at the lakefront of Lake Nahuel.

102. Villa Lago Gutierrez is a small lake lodge on Lake Gutierrez near Bariloche, Argentina.

103. Portrait of a Young Man, painted by Raphael, is believed to be a self-portrait, completed 1513-1514; the Nazis stole it in Poland; many historians believe it to be the most significant painting missing since WWII.

104. Guantanamo Bay is a current US Military base operating on the island of Cuba.

105. During the Vietnam War, the US Navy used small fiberglass boats called Patrol Boat, riverine (PBR) to patrol the Mekong Delta.

106. The Katy Trail is a popular 3.5-mile pedestrian trail built on an old railway corridor. The Katy Trail Ice House is a popular food and beverage establishment on the trail.

107. The eight locations listed are all attractions in each respective city

108. Lago Steffen is located approximately 67 kilometers south of Bariloche

109. Rio Villegas is a small village about 65 kilometers south of Bariloche, near Lago Steffen.

110. Snow White and the Seven Dwarfs was a 1937 animated musical film produced by Walt Disney Productions. It was based on the 1812 German fairy tale by the Brothers Grimm.

111. Br'er Rabbit is a trickster rabbit character in stories written by Joel Chandler Harris. Harris first popularized the Uncle Remus stories highlighting the Br'er rabbit character in 1879/80 after hearing folktales of the black African plantation workers.

112. In 1890, an estimated 2.8 million German-born immigrants lived in the United States. Most were located in the German triangle, which had Cincinnati, Milwaukee, and St. Louis as its three points.

113. The locations listed in the paragraph are all highlights in Cincinnati.

114. Cincinnati Octoberfest started in 1976. It is now considered the largest Octoberfest in the US and is estimated to be the second largest in the world after Munich.

115. Rhinegeist Craft Brewery, located on Elm Street in Cincinnati, was established in 2013.

116. The Chicken Dance oompah song was originally composed by accordion player Werner Thomas from Davos, Switzerland, in the 1950s.

xxx

ACKNOWLEDGMENTS

First, I want to acknowledge my wife, Barb, who always supported me during my insurance career. She encouraged me to write this book and was my first beta reader, reassuring me about the story.

Next, much appreciation to Dana Alioto, a long-time colleague and author of "Hey Nineteen, A Memoir of Growing Up in Milwaukee, Wisconsin," for his outstanding editorial work on the manuscript. He gave me terrific advice regarding the entire publishing process.

My sister, Kathy Barger, a dedicated, gifted student teacher, and literary expert, provided solid advice as a beta reader. I extend special thanks to Garrett Lucas, son-in-law, who also was a beta reader. He and my daughter, Alyssa, sailed for nearly twenty months on a Lagoon 40 sailboat around the Mediterranean, from Gibraltar to the Canary Islands, across the Atlantic Ocean, up the chain of Caribbean Islands, and finally to Annapolis. I had brief experiences on the boat with them. His instruction and adventure served as inspiration for many of the sailing exploits in the book.

I would also like to thank the original owner of the Kay-Gene cottages in Nags Head, North Carolina. Our family vacationed there every summer, approximately 1965-1975. I cannot remember the owner's name. Every summer, he regaled us with stories about the 1940s era, when he would return to open the cottages for summer. He found German cans, wrappers, and cigarettes on the cottage floors. The German sailors discarded these items after coming ashore from their U-boats for rest and relaxation. These stories led me to research U-boats in the Atlantic Ocean, and that research developed into this fictional story.

Many great thanks to the W. H. Wax Publishing, LLC team. They embraced my manuscript and brought it to distribution. Bill Wax did exceptional work designing the book cover and worked tediously on the editing and formatting.

ABOUT THE AUTHOR

Dennis worked for forty-four years in the insurance industry, relocating seven times. He held various executive positions for six insurance companies. After retiring from his executive career, he began a second career as a novelist.

He is married and lives in Duluth, Georgia. He and his wife raised three children, all of whom are now married. They currently have three grandsons.

Dennis is an avid golfer, loves daily walks with his wheaten terrier, and enjoys hiking, woodworking, spending time with friends and family, and traveling with his wife.

He graduated from the University of Cincinnati, earning a BA in English Literature and a minor in Business. He prioritizes God, country, family as values. He believes happiness is achieved though faith, family, and friends.

Order **A SECRET SOLDIER'S CONFESSION** today!
dennisbargerbooks.com

Made in the USA
Columbia, SC
19 December 2024